Library of

Treasure

Library Of Treasure

By

Reba Jean Smith

Lady Jane Chronicles
Book 2

Word of His Mouth Publishers
Mooresboro, NC

All Scripture quotations are taken from the **King James Version** of the Bible.

ISBN: 978-1-941039-34-2

Printed in the United States of America
©2023 Reba Jean Smith

Word of His Mouth Publishers
Mooresboro, NC

www.wordofhismouth.com

Cover photo
https://www.123rf.com/profile_tomertu
Used by permission.

Prologue

From the Library of Secrets
Book 1 of the Lady Jane Chronicles

Reba Jean opened the library door and slid into its amazing vastness. It really was bigger on the inside than it appeared from the outside structure. Lady Jane had told her a few times that even though the first floor was usually all that people saw, it had a multitude of levels and depths. Lady Jane did not like to go to most of the secret places in this library. Reba Jean knew she would need to help Lady Jane navigate through the maze of corridors, construction zones, and concrete-like vaults to bring to fruition this scheme to tell the truth without anyone realizing it was an autobiography.

Chapter 1

The first book was barely in the mail awaiting the publisher when the concept for the second book was already pulsating through her head and heart. She vaulted up the steps to the library in earnest, already distracted by the task ahead. She slid into the library, ignoring the ravishes of the last battle, and spun around the center of the atrium surveying the structure and design elements. She barely noticed Lady Jane and her celestial companions still cleaning up the remnants of the fiery attacks from just that very day.

Reba Jean realized she was holding her breath and exhaled with an audible whoosh. This whole new concept was mind-boggling. The library would never and should never be the same if this new strategy were implemented. Where to start? With a twirl, she ran skippity-hoppity to the Ancient One. The only place for answers and solutions was obvious, at least to her. Flipping reverently through the pages, passages began glowing in gold, their words and message leaping out at her in confirmation of the burgeoning concept.

If the library of our minds was the cache for all our thoughts and the books therein contained all our thoughts from the moment when memory began, could there not be a way to delve even deeper into what we put into our mental libraries? As she pondered this some more, a verse came to mind about "out of the abundance of the heart, the mouth speaketh." She had taught for years that what goes into the mind then enters the heart and is thus acted upon. The familiar adage of "garbage in, garbage out" was fully accurate. What if she turned that around spiritually and only put good thoughts in her library?

Was that possible? The last month had been a daily war of her mind being attacked with abominable wickedness. She had often bowed down in overwhelming defeat only for the verse in James to resonate with the words RESIST the devil and he will flee from you. More often than ever the only word she could cling to in that verse was "resist." She would be bowed over literally screaming that word silently for all the underworld to hear. Not once had she given in to those horrible suggestions that had pierced her peace. The word RESIST was repeated over and over in desperation. Eventually, the temptation or thought would finally subside. Every attack had the essence of her feeling pummeled to the point that she was feeling overwhelmed or overpowered.

Reba Jean was exceedingly tired of the flesh or the devil somehow thinking that these horrific thoughts were a weakness of hers to exploit. Was there something she could do differently to not even have these sorts of attacks? Did other Christians get bombarded daily, sometimes hourly with such abominable thoughts? She truly did understand why some people gave up or gave in or both. They just wanted the attacks to stop! Sadly, they did not understand that the only way to make them stop is by resisting them every single time! Reba Jean's eyes took in the damage displayed throughout the library from these attacks. Lady Jane herself was physically scarred, and there was still so much soot and gaping holes in the fibrous membranes of the library walls.

What if instead of secrets to hide and protect or keep from being exploited by the evil one, she could keep only good thoughts? Could this library of secrets be turned into a different sort of library?

Was it even possible with all the baggage from her past, her penchant for thinking wickedly, or her critical spirit? What sort of things could be stored in the library?

Her eyes dropped down the open page of the Ancient One, and the glowing words caught her eye again. Matthew 12:35, "A good man out of the good treasure of the heart bringeth forth good things: and an evil man out of the evil treasure bringeth forth evil things." Herein lay the new concept. A breeze flipped the pages of the Ancient One and then dissipated as the glowing words from Matthew 6:19-21 caught her attention. "Lay not up for yourselves treasure upon earth, where moth and rust doth corrupt, and where thieves break through and steal: But lay up for yourselves treasures in heaven, where neither moth nor rust doth corrupt, and where thieves do not break through nor steal: For where your treasure is, there will your heart be also."

What if instead of secrets in this library, it was a library of treasure instead? *What sort of treasure do you store in a mental library?* Reba Jean pondered this for a bit, then decided to just start simply. If she treated each thought based on its spiritual value, would that totally change how she thought? Were her thoughts trash or treasure? The time to put this intriguing concept into practice was now. So, when those abominable thoughts came, she would not just resist, but she would be able to deflect and reject them as trash. Looking around the library, she saw books upon books holding trivia and what amounted to just useless trash. This library needed radical renovation!

Lady Jane shook cloying soot off her skirt and stretched her aching muscles. She so wanted to slump in defeat, but there seemed to be an air of expectation drifting through the library toward her. She could almost smell something new. Sniffing the air, she decided to follow her nose as it led her to the Ancient One. She was surprised to see Reba Jean standing in front of the Ancient One; she had not realized her mistress had entered the battlefield. She sensed Goodness and Mercy flanking her as they waited in anticipation. Reba Jean appeared to be deep in thought, and you could almost see the concentration visibly as she meditated on the words from the Ancient One.

Misty tendrils hovered as if awaiting orders or instructions; the golden glitter of the dust motes commenced dancing; the artifacts that had been created and designed in the previous month lent an air of celestial promise and purpose. Reba Jean needed more than just lovely thoughts like buttercups and daisies or the word "Resist" to help her library be spiritually transformed. She needed to start holding herself accountable for every thought. If her works, thusly her actions, were going to be held in a spiritual balance... Where was that passage of Scripture? Ahh, yes, 1 Corinthians 3:13, but it seemed like there was another passage. Reba Jean started searching the pages of the Ancient One. She was sure this concept was from the Lord, but she needed Scripture to confirm it.

She searched through Scripture for what seemed like a long time, reading much but yearning for more. She knew time ran differently in the library, but she sensed that this study was more of a journey and not just an afternoon. Looking up, she saw Lady Jane studying her in the glow emanating off the Ancient One, and she exchanged an inscrutable look with her. Lady Jane had been through so much war and trauma as she lived at ground zero of every spiritual battle that had taken place in the library. Reba Jean realized that maybe Lady Jane needed to truly be a curator, not of a structure holding books, but of treasure and thoughts that had value and were precious enough to keep.

If this had been a library in the outer world, she would have a massive book burning. However, in this library of mental storage, it was time to change the usual habit of displaying or even organizing all the books; instead, more of them needed to be packed away, never to be seen or read again. They amounted to wood, hay, stubble and not to gold, silver, and precious stones. What she had started just a few months ago was now an earnest task to truly have a transformed mind. The Scripture that she had already read seemed to flow through the air on golden beams of light, and the whole library seemed to bask in the celestial light shimmering into every dark, war-torn corner. The sound system began to stream the orchestrated music once again to "Spirit of the Living God Fall Fresh on Me," and a holy hush filled the library.

The two women knelt together and asked the Lord God of Heaven to help them transform this library into a gallery of treasures. "Amazing Grace" burst forth as they worshipped the Lord in that hallowed hall. Eventually, Reba Jean rose and gave Lady Jane a helping hand, as she was still very fragile from her wounds. Reba Jean needed to head back down to the living room, but she was still fully expecting to hear from her Heavenly Father on the way to transform this library of hers into a library of treasures instead of dark, evil secrets.

Chapter 2

The next few weeks were full of stress, changes, challenges, and continued attacks of abominable thoughts. Reba Jean often screamed the word "TREASURE" in her mind during these attacks instead of the word RESIST from that verse in the book of James. It seemed to help as she still struggled with the "why?" of these attacks. She never gave in, but they sure did wear her out. Her blood pressure started spiking, and she often felt cranky. The second book was burning into her brain as the first one seemed to recede. How she longed to start writing and seeing where this literary escapade took her.

Then, just as she felt like she needed to pray for more patience, the publisher contacted her with his approval of her first book! That is right, her first BOOK!!!! She was about to become a published author! She repeatedly thanked the Lord for this confirmation of what He had begun in her just a couple of months ago. Not long after, she was able to sit down with the publisher and work out some details and marketing strategies. She was still the same awkward, often insecure woman who just wanted to lead a quiet, peaceable life in all godliness, but the Lord was choosing her to spread His Word in her much-loved format.

As she pondered this new concept of treating thoughts as if they were treasures to keep and guard, she was reminded of Mary, the mother of Jesus, who "kept all these things, and pondered them in her heart." The next verse that came to mind was, "...Let this mind be in you which was also in Christ Jesus..." She was supposed to have the mind of Christ; that was something to treasure. She was to lay up treasure in heaven, which could only be done if her mind was always on a treasure hunt.

Her preacher gave a message one night that seemed to line up with this pattern of thought. It was on 1 Timothy 6:17-19, but his points grabbed her attention. It was about treasures that money cannot buy: a satisfied mind and a heart that is contented. Words in 1 Peter 1:13 also seemed to reiterate this thought, "Wherefore gird up the loins of your mind, be sober, and hope to the end for the grace that is to be brought unto you at the revelation of Jesus Christ." Gird up the loins of your mind; so many places in Scripture talk about the mind and how important it was to be sober-minded. Surely, what is in our mind and our thoughts is critical to how we live.

Reba Jean continued studying about how to transform her mind based on Scripture through the following days. What sort of things were to be treasured, she wondered? If she could compile a list of treasures to keep in her library, then she could focus on those spiritual treasures, and guarding those treasures would change how the spiritual attacks affected her.

Chapter 3

Lady Jane knew that life was crazy for Reba Jean right now; the puppy had been joined by an exceptionally large dog who had gotten into trouble with another dog. Rescuing animals seemed to be all that Reba Jean did anymore. The stress of it all, along with the world and its sewage spilling out all over, was very taxing. Lady Jane did not see Reba Jean return to the library for quite a few weeks. The atmosphere fluctuated between anticipation and then discouragement that nothing was changing. The misty tendrils, however, did not behave as they usually did. Instead, they seemed bound up or unable to move. The golden dust motes, however, were more prevalent, and the air was often a cloud of lovely glitter caressing everything it touched.

Lady Jane wandered around the library, her eyes taking in the precious artifacts like the crystal water in the fountain, the rugged table and oil lamp, the gossamer table runner, and occasionally, she would catch a glimpse of the beautiful, iridescent blue butterfly as it flitted freely through the aisles. The buzz of the bees from Sir Theo's library was steady, yet there was an undercurrent of anxious anticipation. Hopeful changes were coming to that library as well. Lady Jane decided to peek into Sir Theo's library just to check on him. She realized as she entered his library that he was not there; he had been called in to work. Yet, there on his desk was a book he had received in the mail. Oh, how she rejoiced when she saw it, and happily, she knew that Reba Jean had rejoiced as well. It was a book on prayer, and Sir Theo was reading it. Lady Jane almost sobbed with thankfulness.

Reba Jean began to write her second book in earnest; her husband said it was not a bad hobby to have. If it was lucrative, then that would be a bonus. As the lovely sounds of orchestrated hymns flowed through the air, she felt her heart and mind settle from all the recent chaos and stress. The words flowed as they had for the first book, but this time it felt more like a journey for her spiritual maturity. If her mind was a library, and thus, a library of treasure, what sort of treasures were to be kept there? Philippians 4:8 told of the things we should think about; other Scriptures talked about the thoughts of God Himself.

She continued to search through Scripture, knowing that too often her thoughts were vanity and not of value. Her first treasure was salvation; the only other treasure she could take to Heaven was whomever she led to salvation in the Lord. So, salvation and witnessing were to be treasured in her library. Music that pleased and praised the Lord was of immense value; a song of praise and worship to her Creator was a precious treasure to keep. A thought caught her attention, and she rushed up to the library to look for a book that had not been opened or written in enough.

Lady Jane heard the door swoosh open, and she looked up from her musings to see Reba Jean hurry into the stacks like a woman on a mission. Rummaging through shelves, brushing off dusty titles, she was on a treasure hunt for an important book. Oh, where was it?!! Reba Jean felt panic increasing as she ran down the aisles, her fingers skimming over raised embossed titles, searching for that one specific title. It was not in the rows of books; Reba Jean stopped, inhaled, and tried to think where this book could be. Why hadn't it been out where it could be written in every day?

Reba Jean jerked with the realization that the book was on her desk in the den downstairs! She had no excuse not to be writing daily in this book. With a mad rush, she dashed back down the stairs rifling through all the unorganized ledgers and notebooks on her desk until she found it. This special book that she had entitled The Blessing Book was precious to her. Sadly, only a few of its pages had been used to list all the things she was thankful for. Thanksgiving and a grateful heart were valuable;

with the book securely in hand, she once again ascended the steps to the library.

Lady Jane raised a bemused eyebrow at Reba Jean as she nearly tumbled into the library, going faster than her feet could carry her. Reba Jean brushed past her bemused friend and placed the book on a side table in the atrium. Then she turned to Lady Jane and beckoned her closer to better hear what she was about to say. "Lady Jane, we have been through so much together. It seems like the attacks lately are stronger and more wicked, and with my huge guilt complex, I wonder if most of these attacks are somehow my fault," Reba Jean announced with a determined air. "The Lord has impressed upon me to write a second book about this library but with the focus being on thoughts that have value, that should be guarded like you would guard treasures."

Lady Jane tilted her head sideways as she listened to Reba Jean explain the premise of the new book, but furthermore, the new purpose of this library. The concept was mind-blowing, no pun intended. So, instead of a gazillion thoughts flying around and the odd shoe dangling or the trains running off their tracks, it would hopefully be more like a castle designed for treasure that was befitting the Royalty Who lived there or visited. Oh, surely King Abba and Lord Rabboni would be pleased with this treasure hunt!

Reba Jean showed Lady Jane her blessing book where she recorded everything that she was thanking God for, and then together, they sang a song of praise. As they sang, the pages of the Ancient One flipped open to the Book of Psalms, the hymnbook of the Scriptures. Golden dust motes formed into musical notes, and you could literally see the music as they sang. Oh, what a grand start to the transformation of the library and its two earthly inhabitants.

As life would happen, Reba Jean never stayed in the library long enough to see real changes. The more she concentrated on reading the Scriptures and hunting for mental treasures to keep, she realized that the attacks had abated. Perhaps, the secret was more time spent meditating on God's Word rather than questioning why the attacks happened. Trying to be what most people would consider normal, she agreed to yet another task, a level of responsibility that she was not truly sure she should do. After saying yes, she received discouragement from family members instead of support. Her husband knew of her physical limitations and how the situation did not seem to be very conducive to her sanity. He suggested some necessary guidelines; another confidante suggested boundaries that should be set.

Feeling the weight of the zoo she was now keeping and the upcoming changes that weighed on her mind, Reba Jean began praying in earnest for God to somehow resolve the muddle she had gotten into by trying to be nice. She also prayed that if God did want her to do all these things that He would give her that extra measure of grace she would so desperately need. The book was burning in her mind, but her body was overwhelmed by the stress, and she spent most of the week in bed.

Was it wrong to want peace, quiet, and time to reflect or write a book? Reba Jean longed to go back to the library and begin renovating it. Lady Jane deserved some much-needed rest as well. Ignoring the dogs, the thoughts that tried to stress her out, the waiting for prayers to be answered, and the various issues her body was trying to distract her with, she strode up the stairs to the library.

Opening the door, she stood at the entrance and just watched to see what was going on inside. The lovely sounds of orchestrated hymns soothingly caressed her weary mind, and she almost collapsed in relief. It was relatively peaceful right now. Twilight filtered through the crystal blue panes of the windows, and the blue butterfly could be seen flitting on an unseen breeze. Babbling sounds came from the fountain of living water, and a gentle mist of golden glitter settled down like a cape around her shoulders. With an exhaled sigh of relief, Reba Jean wandered through the atrium, soaking in the peace that God have given her mind.

Lady Jane heard that sigh, and with a happy heart, she went to meet her mistress on the far side of the atrium. They hugged each other tightly for a few minutes, and then together, they strode down the corridor. Golden light warmly glowed from the oil lamp as they passed by it sitting on the rugged table. The table was still blocking the entrance to the Crimson Vault. Following the corridor, they stopped by the three golden tiles on the floor and then giggled together companionably as they saw that the wall had been removed and the corridor continued down further to a softly lit nursery at the end. Reba Jean took a moment to thank the Lord for the continued health of her grandbaby that was still in the womb.

Was answered prayer a treasure to keep in the library? The continued strains of the music embraced them as they continued to tour the library. Sir Theo's library was quiet; he was once again at work. The book on prayer was moved to another room that he often spent a lot of time in as well. Reba Jean let the peace of the library soak into her very soul. Lady Jane closed her eyes as the serenity of the moment brought healing to the ravages of her mind and spirit. Peace was most assuredly treasured in this library.

Together, the two women sat down on the floor near the Ancient One and discussed library renovations. Were the books to be removed and hidden away? Maybe good memories could stay? Was this something they were to physically do, or was it more just focusing so much on the treasures of the Word of God that the books themselves would fade from view? Reba Jean realized the puppy had been quiet for a long time, which was not natural, and she ran downstairs to check on it. With relief and a heartfelt thank you to the Lord, she saw it was on the couch being good while she had been in the library. With that bit of relief, she ran back to the library. Oh, how good it was to see progress being made toward a real transformation.

Lady Jane's eyes grew enlarged as she felt the atmosphere in the library mellow out, and the fibrous walls seemed to solidify into something reminiscent of a castle fortress. The music permeated the entire library, and they closed their eyes and let the hymns of worship wash over them. A holy Presence filled the library, and the women realized that the Overseer had joined them because of their worship to the Heavenly King. Reba Jean felt goosebumps on her arms, and she shivered in awe and delight as she savored the moment.

Transformation would take time, work, dedication, and consistent persistence. Not every moment was going to be this peaceful, so she decided to treasure this moment as well. With that thought, the glitter of the golden dust motes formed themselves into musical notes, and she watched as a beautiful chamber was created off one side of the atrium. Lining the walls were golden lyrics of well-loved hymns, and many instruments appeared, all composing a melody of praise to the Lord. Over the arched entrance the golden words from Psalm 96 etched themselves, tracing downward along the sides of the archway and spilling along and across the adjoining wall.

Lady Jane clapped her hands in childish glee as she saw the new chamber of praise; no more would she have to hope and yearn for the orchestrated music to stream forth from the sound system in the living room. She could enter this chamber of praise right here in the library! As if on cue, "Holy, Holy, Holy" began to stream through the chamber causing the whole library to radiate with the attitude of praise and worship. Reba Jean heard the Holy Spirit remind her that Philippians 4:8 spoke of praise as one of the things worth thinking about. With that verse running through her mind, she thought she needed to do a deeper study of what those words meant since each of those were potential treasures for the library!

The inhabitants of Reba Jean's pet menagerie began to get restless for her attention, and it was going to be necessary to return to the rest of the house. With a deep reluctance, Reba Jean hugged Lady Jane and left the library to attend to life as she now knew it. However, it was becoming more reassuring that this new quest for treasure was going to make an incredibly dramatic difference in her life and library. What sort of treasures would she find as she truly studied Philippians 4:8 and applied it to her quest? She did not want hidden treasures; she wanted them prominently displayed but also guarded and kept for daily use.

Reba Jean went downstairs and posted a question on social media "Can you truly do something without thinking?" Not sure what she had expected for feedback, but most people believed that you would, could, and will do many things without thinking about them. She understood this mentality, yet it concerned her. Were too many of God's people wandering through life on auto pilot, going through the motions, just existing instead of purposefully living for the Lord with thoughtful intent? Mulling this over, Reba Jean concluded that she needed to be more conscious of what she was doing, and the reason she was doing it.

Someone had told her that very day that they needed a friend with wisdom. She was not sure if that quite depicted her, but she was grateful that they had equated her in that category. This thought about wisdom led her to start a search for Scripture about wisdom. Excitedly she realized that this was another treasure to add to her library! She had not even thought about that; oh, how exhilarating to see the treasures increasing! Each one of them would take a lifetime to collect and utilize and here she had already found praise, thankfulness, wisdom, and worship, and she had not even finished studying Philippians 4:8.

Recognizing that she had discovered these treasures, she also knew that she was not just to collect or hoard them; she had to put them to use for the kingdom of God. A verse came to mind,

Colossians 3:16, that seemed to summarize her recent treasure hunt. "Let the word of Christ dwell in you richly in all wisdom; teaching and admonishing one another in psalms and hymns and spiritual songs, singing with grace in your hearts to the Lord." That was her treasure hunt thus far in a nutshell.

Where else would her treasure hunt take her? What dangers and pitfalls would try to ensnare her along the way? It is not that she was wanting to borrow trouble; it just always seemed to find her. She did not want to think about what might happen to trip her up. She just wanted to revel in the newness of this quest. She mused on these things as she brushed the hair of the big dog outside. Her friend, Sunshine, often expected her to have a spiritual application handy for anything she did. This time was no different as she brushed away the abundant dog hair to rid the dog of excess hair and dirt that would only hinder it from cooling off on these sweltering summer days. The verse from Hebrews 12:1 came to mind "…let us lay aside every weight, and the sin which doth so easily beset us."

Her husband texted her to say that his sugar was probably high, and she recommended flushing his system with water. This, too, had a spiritual application. When we are overloaded with the toxins that hinder our flesh, we need to flush our hearts and bodies with the water of the Word of God. With this thought, Reba Jean mentally committed to hopefully finishing this new book in the next month. The first one took less than an actual month to write, so hopefully this one could be done in the same amount of time. The upcoming months would present an overwhelming challenge to her time and temperament unless the Lord intervened, as she was now praying that He would.

All this thought and talk about water made her thirsty, so she took the time to drink a glass of water as she waited for her husband to return home from work. Letting the soft strains of the hymns seep into her consciousness, she tried to hold onto the peace that it offered. Dogs barking, cats hissing and meowing, and her stomach churning, all tried to rob her of the progress she had made. The flesh was weak, but her desire to be strong in the Lord and in the power of His might was renewed after her visit to the library earlier.

Chapter 4

Reba Jean wrote some more in her book while she waited for her husband's return. The plot was not all sorted out in her head this time, but she did not let that bother her. She may hit writer's block on this one, but only until the Lord revealed the next words to write. Oh, she knew this book was also from the Lord, again, maybe it was only for her benefit. The publisher wanted her to market the books; he did not realize how daunting this was to her. She did not crave attention or the limelight, hence the pseudonym. The use of the pseudonym was also freeing, because if you did not truly know her you would not expect this book to be written by little old Reba Jean. Those who were characters within the book would only realize it if they read it and caught the significant clues.

Only Lady Constance and Mardie knew about these books, and that they were enveloped within the plot. Reba Jean annoyingly fiddled with the spacing on the paragraph she was trying to write. This was, of course, better than doing a handwritten manuscript. But the software was difficult to control at times. She almost giggled as she could draw spiritual applications and comparisons to each of these situations. Sunshine would just give her a look or a laugh, who knew. Then she realized that she had somehow clicked overwrite mode; no wonder she was having so many issues with editing her words. Overwrite mode, now there, too, was an interesting spiritual application to ponder. Reba Jean pondered that for a minute, as she listened to the hymns, the big dog barking, the puppy whining, and took a moment to just thank God silently for overwriting her life.

The big dog was barking yet again. She knew this could be a ploy for attention, but you just never knew if there was something else out there. Reba Jean went outside to sit with the big dog for a while. Her container garden came into view, and she saw the weeds growing amidst the squash plants. She could pull the weeds, but the squash plants were using them as anchors as they took over the whole garden instead of the weeds. She pondered this for a time. She had weeds to remove in her life, but she also needed to be like the squash plants and if the weeds were not removed just grow over them and smother them. Her attention was then diverted to the seeds that had been sown by the wayside and now she had a pumpkin plant growing in her yard. She reminded herself to grow where she was planted and to blossom and flourish. This night was most definitely a night of spiritual application and meditation on God's Word.

Leaving the big dog alone again, she prayed once again that God would help her with the issues that she was potentially facing in the months ahead due to her own penchant for trying to fix everyone's problems. She was thankful that every time a thought came to mind, she had a Scripture verse to apply to it. "Oh, may every night be like this," she breathed in prayer. The puppy was making loud noises with the toy it was playing with, the big dog was finally silent for the moment, the music was still soothing her soul as she still waited for her husband to get home so she could go to bed knowing he was safe. Her stomach was still upset; she was not sure if she was still letting stress affect her physically or if her new eating habits in hopes of losing weight were messing with her.

Reba Jean had thought she was just being lazy, so she, of course, agreed to do things that ended up being physically overwhelming to her because she thought she was supposed to say "yes." She did not want to be thought of as selfish; the words of Proverbs 31 often ran through her mind. Here she was, yet again, just physically unable to keep up with all the demands that her current circumstances were leveling at her—the big dog for example. She was told just yesterday that the dog viewed her as

26

livestock. She knew she had outwardly handled that remark well, but inwardly she felt like it was adding insult to injury. Livestock, pshaw, and then she was told by another younger person that she needed to practice for having a grandbaby. These younger ones meant well, maybe they did not mean to sound as thoughtless as they did, but again maybe they were truly doing and saying things without thinking.

These were weeds that she was either going to pull or use to grow around; she intended to be a squash plant and not a shrinking violet. However, she had a feeling she needed to be more of a touch-me-not mimosa: hardy, protective, and invasive. Did others look for spiritual applications in their daily lives? This was a treasure to her; hmmm, a treasure, now that sounded like something she could keep in her library of treasures as well.

The next day, Reba Jean lounged around, mentally puttering with memories and thoughts over current events as she did some minimal housework. The world was, as always, a very volatile place to live. There were so many dangers and pitfalls to watch out for, wisdom and discernment were paramount to navigate the treacherous seas of life. Thoughts paraded through her mental calisthenics, and if it had been a month ago, she would have been worried about the library's reaction to this bout of randomness. However, since shoring up the walls of the library into solid rock-like sturdiness, the thoughts could not rampage around willy-nilly like they used to do.

With that measure of fortitude in place, Reba Jean revisited the library to putter around in there as well while she had a few moments to spare. She met Lady Jane in the atrium by the fountain and together they walked to the music room to inhale its essence of praise. After a few moments, they continued arm in arm to the dream room. This room had been created a few short months prior, but Reba Jean was not satisfied with it. Her dreams of late had been the usual nonsense, and now mostly forgettable. This was progress, so Reba Jean decided a whole room devoted to them was not necessary. She stood there with her hands on her hips, trying to decide what to do with the contents of the dream room. Lady Jane waited in silence, just thankful that she no longer had to deal with Reba Jean's dreams or nightmares. A misty tendril dropped down and tapped Reba Jean on the shoulder; mystified, she looked around as it pointed to some strongboxes in the side corridor. Oh, what a great idea! Reba Jean opened her arms, gathered up the fragments of dreams that were all hazy and blurry and stuffed them into one of the strongboxes. With a slam of the lid and a turn of the key, she locked away all the dreams that used to ravage the library at night.

Reba Jean then eyed those misty tendrils, those electrical synapses of thought that dangled everywhere in the library. She realized that before, they had little discipline and often were used to print thoughts in books that should have never even been recognized or brought to fruition. The walls of the library looked like the strong stone of a fortified castle; could not the misty tendrils be transformed into something also secure and strong? Pulling a misty tendril that was nearby, she fingered it and then had an interesting thought. The misty tendril felt that thought and with a recoiling jerk, it reconnected to the network of the tendrils throughout the library. What happened next left the women gob smacked. The network of misty tendrils wove themselves into a mesh of chainmail that covered the entire ceiling of the library. She did not necessarily want the proverbial steel trap of a mind, but one that was not subject to the wiles of the evil one would be a definite improvement.

The two women hugged each other as they realized that although the fiery darts would constantly barrage the library, maybe only a few of them would find their way through the doubled fortifications that were now in place. The library of secrets was changing into a library of treasure: strong, secure, and sanctified. Reba Jean decided to just see what would happen to the rows upon rows of books of her stored thoughts and memories; hopefully, she would not have to do much with them.

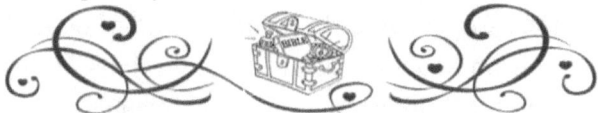

Meanwhile, Mr. Insidious had been promoted for his continual barrage on the library. His army of minions had done well, though there had been some failed skirmishes here and there. Overall, however, the fiery darts and vile wicked thoughts were never short on supply. Captain Insidious, as he was now known, had also promoted Insecurity and his various other villainous creatures. Then, something odd happened. The usual vile, wicked, abominable thoughts and suggestions did not seem to have the usual effect or result. In fact, the resistance was stronger than in just days past. Captain Insidious saw that his constant barrage did not seem to be getting anywhere.

He decided to send out some scouts to see if they could find a way into the library or at least peer through a weak spot and see what was happening to their lifelong soirees. Captain Insidious could just pick some volunteers from the slimy-smelling minions that shrieked around him, but just maybe he needed to be a bit judicious in his selection. Tapping a claw-like finger on his cheek, he felt the black ooze run down his cheek as he scratched himself. Who would make the best scouts in this situation? His eyes squinted nearly shut when an ingenious idea occurred to him; he would commandeer a few scouts from the Chameleon Company. This elite squad was trained to just blend in and appear to be whatever they needed to be for a time. They were often embedded in the churches and spiritually strong communities to appear to be just like the saints. They would then gather information or sow discord or even cause apathy.

Selecting a few scouts from this undercover squad, Captain Insidious dispatched them with the mission. Captain Insidious was used to the long game as always, so he knew this could take some time before he was able to plot a new barrage on the library and its occupants. In the meantime, he sent in a dragonfly drone to peer into the windows; he often used social media or television to get an idea of what weaknesses to exploit. Reba Jean was still immersed in both avenues of potential brainwashing. And even though she tried to distance herself from those, she was always lured back in. The dragonfly drone, however, just resembled a dragonfly and seemed banal. After a few tries, the dragonfly returned to report that the library looked vastly different than it had just weeks before. However, it had been able to also view the living room, and that looked more chaotic and just possibly easier to assault.

Captain Insidious gathered his strategists armed with this new suggestion of assaulting the living room and, thus, ultimately, entering the library. What tools could they use in this arena? It was soon obvious, just by paying a bit of attention to his quarry, that stress, family obligations, and the need to feel like a "good Christian" would make for good weapons at hand. With hideous glee distorting his evil features even more, he sounded out the charge to his infantry.

Chapter 5

Reba Jean was struggling with all the stress of the zoo, the work, and financial issues, and on top of those, she felt obligated to accept another overwhelming responsibility without praying or talking with her husband first. She began to try to pray her way out of what her mouth had gotten her into.

Sunday came around, and she asked the Lord to give her an answer that He was at least listening and would help her in His time. A traveling preacher delivered that answer through Psalm 46, "Be still and Know that He is God." She was not very patient, she knew, so waiting for God to work it out was usually extremely hard. However, she was reminded that her husband had told her often to just take one day at a time instead of fretting over the upcoming months ahead. This was something she needed to work on every day.

Lady Jane got a missive from Lady Constance that set her nerves jangling, but they both agreed that, despite varied opinions on the current events, Lord Rabboni was coming soon to gather His bride. She tried to remember to keep her focus on King Abba and not on what the wicked ones were trying to do around her and Reba Jean. Lady Jane had listened to Lady Constance read an excerpt from Reba Jean's first book, and her voice inflections were spot on. It gave her a delicious chill to hear the book come to life with the right narrator. Lady Jane hoped Reba Jean would use Lady Constance further in producing her books, if possible. Sir Theo had even suggested that Lady Constance narrate the books into an audio format. Her personality was such, he declared, that it would make the book even more exciting by hearing it read aloud.

Reba Jean kept telling herself to stop thinking and planning and to just wait on God. She found this was not something she was used to doing. As she scrolled through social media, a post too long to share was full of nuggets. It reminded her that even the small answers to prayer could be considered as treasure. Of course, anything with the word treasure leaped out at her these days, so she added that to her treasure hunt checklist. With that thought in mind, she catapulted to her feet and dashed up the steps to the library. Carefully securing the door behind her, she ran to a few large chests, and selecting one, she used it as a table. She then looked up at the golden dust motes, and they sifted down to her, allowing her to form them into a beautiful gold quill. Plucking some pages from some books, she formed them into a scroll and began to write down in beautifully scrolling script the list of treasures that she had or hoped to acquire.

Her salvation, answered prayers, songs of praise, a peaceful mind, a stilled heart. These treasures already obtained were huge just in themselves. The words gave her a great pause, and she re-read them. Each of these treasures were worth their own galleries in the library. She really felt like she had just barely scratched the surface of each of these treasures. Philippians 4:8 ran through her mind yet again; this was what she was to be thinking about, not stress or concerns or her penchant for getting in over her head. What other treasures should she be searching for?

Captain Insidious felt a strong ripple run through his troop; there seemed to be an undercurrent of surprise at the strength they were met with. The intel was such that just stress and family obligations would not win. Captain Insidious gave a disgusted laugh at the ineptitude of some of the foot soldiers under his command. He was not dissuaded; persistence was the strongest strategy. He sent Insecurity into the fray, reminding him to use his weapons of body image and social status and target his assault on her appearance and sleep. He was aware that if Reba Jean did not sleep, she and Lady Jane would suffer. The weaker he could make them, the simpler it would be to not just overwhelm them but overcome them.

Reba Jean sensed that even though the attacks seemed to be less than before, she was not free of them. Strengthening the library was vital, and focusing on what she was supposed to be thinking about and waiting on God to move in His time and will was more like just the fundamentals. It was most likely that this was a lull in the middle of the hurricane.

She descended from the library and sat outside with the dogs to ponder these thoughts. Witnessing was not a treasure she had much of in her library. Oh, she had tried with the neighbors, and she was trying with another young lady, but their hearts were not open. She had always comforted herself that she was just sowing or watering, and God would give the increase, but sometimes she wondered if she was doing it wrong. She did not, however, want to sound like a used car salesman, so therein lay the crux of the issues. Just maybe, however, witnessing was one of those treasures that she would not necessarily see until she got to Heaven.

Reba Jean ruminated, letting her thoughts wander where they would, and again, she felt like she was not living life, just trying to survive. God wanted her to have life and have it more abundantly, yet she only seemed to have overwhelming stress. Many verses dealt with this, but how to achieve the abundant life still seemed a mystery to her. She pursed her lips and felt her face grimace, features that displayed a middle line somewhere between discouragement and a resolute expression of plodding along. Her leg began its fidgeting bounce, something she disdained in others, but in private she did it herself when she was anxious.

Seriously though, if she did not have the puppy or the big dog, or do manual labor, or say yes to things that she did not want to do, would she be happier? Would she feel more of the joy of the Lord? Were these things the issue? Mentally listing all the possible burdensome issues, she had to wonder if she should just make herself enjoy the life that she had instead of wishing for an escape. Distracted by a phone call from her husband, she had to set aside any further contemplation as supper had to be started, and she had to deal with the reality of the tasks her life demanded of her. Thoughts of "what if" were not too far away from her mind, though, and as the puppy once again demanded attention, she was left pondering how to have joy in the midst of it all.

As the week came to an end, Reba Jean had a serious case of her "want-to" being broken. Even writing her book was something she was reluctant to do, yet some serious psychoanalyzing was still taking place. She could honestly say that if the zoo had not increased and she had not felt obligated to say "yes" to extra responsibility, she would have less stress. The heart of the matter was that by agreeing to take on more responsibility, she was putting the burden of responsibility on her own shoulders that someone else had abdicated. That burden was just that, a burden that seemed too heavy to bear. Even her shoulders slumped under the weight. Not until the message that morning on the radio had come on had she realized that she was fretting. Listening to that message and seeing posts on the same subject on social media, she knew that she needed to "Be Still," and God would work it out.

Shivering with the emotional battle, Reba Jean struggled to give those burdens over to God and practice patience. In addition to the burdens that she had taken responsibility for, her family was planning a reunion of sorts in a couple of months. Shivering violently, Reba Jean realized that this whole family business still affected her to the very core. She always started shaking every time she thought or spoke of her family issues. With a burst of defiance, Reba Jean strode to the tea kettle to start some tea for comfort and warmth.

The Holy Spirit had been constantly reminding her to figure out the prayer closet issue she had yet once again. Oh, she prayed very often, but not in the prayer closet anymore since the puppy would bark to distraction if she walked out of sight.

Yet, there was progress, for the puppy was learning to nap by itself at times while she was writing or studying. Reba Jean paused to collect her thoughts and nerves as she wanted to just soak in the lack of things to do this last week of the month. The next few months were going to be overwhelming unless God intervened or He just strengthened her. Waiting for the water for the tea to boil in the kettle, Reba Jean let her mind wander off into nothingness. Maybe she would just take her cup of tea up to the library and share it with Lady Jane. The library seemed more of a sanctuary these days compared to the living room. Many verses she had read in her research about the treasures she should be seeking had her realizing that the living room was extremely important to protect if the library was to stay secure.

Chapter 6

Additional scouts returned with more news for Captain Insidious; the family gathering was confirmed, and they had a date. Also, VBS was coming up soon, and everyone knew what havoc that always wreaked with Reba Jean! The troop was giddy with ghoulish glee until a whiny, little voice reminded them that last year had not been a year for celebration—Reba Jean had her first good year in a decade! Also, they needed to remember that the very source of the usual discord was not going to be there this year. The troop pounced on the bearer of such news and pummeled him in their hot displeasure.

Captain Insidious snapped the whip that he had received upon his promotion and drew the snarling horde's attention back to him. "We will just have to devise new mischief, discord, ego-centric interruptions…" His voice trailed off in thought; oh, this would be the perfect opportunity for the chameleon company to worm their way into the fracas. The chameleon crew would act like they were helping and serving the assumed Master, but the Evil One was their true master.

Captain Insidious had a bounce to his step as he began to scheme and strategize; the assault was going to be two-fold. Every day he would make sure that doubt, insecurity, anxiety, and stress ate away at the fortifications, and then with the bigger skirmishes already planned for those specific dates, he could mount an all-out attack. Oh, he was aware that the Creator King claimed the soul of that worm of a girl, but he knew he could destroy her body, mind, and spirit, often without even directly touching her. She might think she was strong in the power of that Heavenly might, but he could distract her and cut her off from any help or hope. He had done it repeatedly; this time would be no different and no less satisfying, either.

Reba Jean took her peppermint tea up the staircase to the library; her shakes had lessened as she had distracted herself by puttering in the kitchen as the tea steeped. Entering the library, she was immediately and lovingly encased in beautiful melodies of praise as they swirled through the whole library. She closed her eyes and felt her very soul fill with hope and help. Who knew that the library could be an escape, a sanctuary? She soaked in the peace that she had not been feeling in the rest of her house. The steam ascended out of her mug and seemed to spell out the words "Be Still" in a banner over her head. With a sob, Reba Jean sank to the floor, and her soul cried out to the Lord above, thanking Him for the reminder that He cared, that He was in control, and that He would carry her through these next few months.

Lady Jane glanced up as the air in the library changed; it was Reba Jean entering. Sniffing the air, she smelled peppermint tea wafting her way. Following her nose to the atrium, she looked for Reba Jean. Oh no! With a hurried gait, she swished her way to her mistress, wrapped the sobbing form of the beloved woman to her, she prayed to Lord Rabboni for help, health, and hope for her. After a few moments of silent prayer for each other, they raised their heads, wiped away tears and sniffles, and smiled shakily at each other.

Something tapped her leg; Reba Jean looked down to see the puppy had joined her in the library! Not sure whether to be frustrated or amused, she sent the puppy outside only to have it rejoin her again. This was going to become yet another issue if that persistent puppy was going to constantly crave attention. The music changed in the library, and it was not nearly as soothing. Oh, it was a worship song, but it did nothing for her right then. With a determined air, she went to the music room after distracting the puppy with its toys and changed the music back to the orchestrated hymns that seemed like such a balm to her wounded psyche.

Then together, the two women sat down in companionable silence and slowly sipped the fragrant peppermint tea sweetened only with honey. Words were not uttered aloud, but much seemed to be communicated between them silently as they seemingly read each other's thoughts and feelings.

The puppy soon tired of entertaining itself and begged and whined to be held, as usual. Sometimes, Reba Jean mused, Christians or even just humans could be aptly compared to different dog temperaments. Not sure she should explore those parallels all that deeply, she tucked the thought away to remind herself not to be like the dogs that she was now responsible for. Her dogs exhibited fear, anxiety, and discontent and demanded frequent attention. Reba Jean knew her underlying issues were just these same traits!

With a sigh, she gathered her unfinished mug of tea, embraced Lady Jane, and took the recalcitrant puppy down the stairs to the living room. That moment of brief healing had helped, but oh, how she had just longed to soak in the comforting essence of the newly fortified library. With a flop, she landed on the sofa and set her mug down on the side table. Staring off into nothing, she tried not to think or feel anything. The puppy shivered—it did not have the comfort of hot tea—so with a mixed sigh of frustration and compassion, she retrieved the recently laundered puppy blanket and together they curled up on the couch for the next couple of hours. She was probably way too similar to this puppy in more ways than she wanted to speculate.

Hours later, after supper, a taxing walk with the young lady she was witnessing to, tending to the dogs, and a long soak in the tub, Reba Jean felt the strong conviction that she needed to get in her prayer closet. There was no reason to wait until tomorrow; her husband was holding the sleeping puppy. As she tried to practice sitting still and listening if God wanted to speak to her, she knew she needed to open her blessing book and record her blessings. After a few long moments of one-sided conversation, but also the determination on how to proceed the next day when it was time for her devotions and prayer time with the puppy around, she went to her desk and opened the copy of the blessing book that she kept there. Her heart was thankful to the Lord for all the blessings she inscribed on that page. It strengthened her, and although she did not receive any sort of epiphany, that did not discourage her in her quest to be still and know that He is God.

During her walk with the young lady, it was suggested that besides fretting, it might be that she was resentful of all the abdicated responsibility that was thrust upon her. The thought bothered her; she had hoped she was not resentful, but she needed to make sure she was not, even if it was "natural" to feel that. In the continued stillness, she confessed this possibility to the Lord and asked for His forgiveness in case that was the root cause of her fretting. Reba Jean let the stillness of the house settle over her with a heart of thankfulness that for the moment it was calm.

Lady Jane felt that things were more settled in the living room than they had been a few hours before. The library was still, except for the hum from Sir Theo's library drifting into hers. It was surreal not to have the misty tendrils recording every thought or idea as they had all her life. To see them in their intricately woven pattern overhead gave her a feeling of security and a sense that things were at least under a semblance of control. Oh sure, Reba Jean had a few fried and loose synapses here and there that dangled down and caused issues occasionally that typically came with age and stress. Lady Jane just went around tucking them back in and tying them together so they wouldn't short-circuit the rest of the library. She took a moment to just stand still and soak in the calm and peace that descended from above and within.

Meanwhile, Captain Insidious had a brief staff meeting. He had sent in a member of the chameleon company in the form of a young lady who was becoming Reba Jean's confidante. However, he was getting undercurrents that Reba Jean was aware she was a chameleon and was not as easily fooled as he hoped. However, his chameleon had reported that the seed or suggestion of resentment had been sown, and that was a small victory that he could build upon, regardless. Rubbing his nubby chin, he knew he had a good thing going by just keeping the zoo stirred up, the husband cranky, and the stress overwhelming. The long game would prove who was the winner.

Reba Jean wasn't aware of the mechanisms of the underworld; she was thankful that the abominable attacks seemed over. However, she was also aware that this brief lull in the storm was just a warning that one was brewing. She needed to take this time and fortify her library and her living room. Those rooms were so intertwined in the deepest ways imaginable; it was paramount that she heed the Word of God and guard her heart and her mind. Should she go up to the library tonight? Had Lady Jane enjoyed her peppermint tea in peace? Feeling uncertain, Reba Jean decided to stay where she was and just enjoy the stillness. The only noise was the air conditioner and her husband's tutorial as he studied for his upcoming exam. She had been tempted to turn on the television, but it somehow seemed like it would ruin the moment. It would be bedtime soon, and she needed her sleep. She knew she wanted to stay away from over-the-counter sleep aids, so she determined she would look up those breathing exercises that helped before she got the puppy.

Chapter 7

Reba Jean halfway grimaced, as she ruminated about her walk tonight with the young lady, and it was almost laughable when she suggested that Reba Jean try a controversial oil to help her sleep. She thought she had handled it well. However, this young lady, claiming to be saved, believed that drinking and even being hungover was okay, and now the suggestion of using this oil called this claim into question. Yes, Reba Jean prayed for this young lady daily to truly know Jesus and to know that she was most likely lost. However, there were many people that named the Name of Christ and yet indulged in the very things that the Bible warned against. It made her heart hurt, hoping these people were really saved and not blinded by their own selfish carnality.

Reba Jean wrapped her arms around herself and thought about her book. It clearly had a different tone about it, yet still written in much the same style. However, she felt like there was maybe an air of detachment emanating from it. She re-read a few paragraphs and thought it sounded all right; maybe it would get better as she went along. A burst of strong men's voices singing about God needing a few good men came from her husband's office. He turned on his own style of praise music; she loved it when he did this. It seemed rare these days.

Ah, this stillness was such a balm to her; it felt so unexpected and out of the new normal. With that thought, she bowed her heart and thanked the Lord for just a night of serenity, song, and strength.

It was time to start getting the house ready for the night and to find those breathing exercises in hopes she could sleep quickly and completely tonight. One of the cats decided it, too, was ready for bedtime, albeit early. With another heart-flung whisper of gratitude to the Lord, Reba Jean arose to tend to the house.

Reba Jean re-read the last paragraph she had written a few days prior and thought about how much had transpired that needed to be analyzed, filtered, discarded, or maybe kept. She wasn't sure how to organize them all in a concise fashion, as she was still ruminating over it all. That little seed of resentment definitely had become a blossom in her mental garden. Even as she recognized it and confessed it, there it was again, rearing its stubborn head throughout the day. She felt frustration mount and knew it was a by-product of resentment. Was it possible to resent resentment? Yes, but now how to get rid of it completely?

She had the opportunity to check on previous students and to hear that the recent graduates seemed to be doing well and flourishing in their library tasks. The current group of students were the usual mixed bag of emotional creatures that needed spiritual and mental guidance every day. However, she found that the seeds of resentment were prevalent in these young librarians. Since it was drawn to her attention about her own situation, she was apt to notice it in others. Was her own battle with resentment oozing onto those around her?

Her husband was a prime example of this query. Just last evening he acknowledged that he was finally aware of how self-centered and self-serving he was. Yet, he didn't know if he had the energy to try to change that about himself. Just this morning, his lack of memory was blamed on her lack of communication. Resentment blossomed forth and caused a rift in their fellowship.

Resentment and frustration seemed to be made of the same ilk and smelled of the underworld from whence they sprang forth. Reba Jean felt as if the claw-like fingers of Insidious of old were trailing down her psyche. She rubbed her temples as she

44

struggled to fight this battle of wills. The abominable suggestions had pretty much ceased as she had resisted them, but this felt like a battle from the beginning of time against pride. Is that not where resentment springs forth? Reba Jean came to a mental and physical stop as she examined this thing that might have been birthed from the ancient first sin of all. No verses about resentment seemed to come to mind, but the Scriptures were chock full of verses upon verses about pride. If she confessed pride and repented of it, would resentment flee?

Captain Insidious clasped his clawed hands in devilish delight; the stronger temptation had been defeated, so he had resorted to the basics. Just simple seeds that were planted by the chameleon scouts were blossoming into rotten, ingloriously stinking fruit. *Back to basics is often the best way to defeat a stronger opponent*, he wrote down in his briefing to the unholy authorities whom he served. Even though he knew that Reba Jean recognized it for what it was, she seemed powerless to resist or flee. He clenched his claws together and twisted them abruptly as if he was snapping off her head, and then cackled with pride as he felt power race through his ghoulish frame. He might not win the final war, but he sure could win some battles and cause her to suffer greatly for getting him thrown out of his library.

Lady Jane climbed onto the top of the old, rugged table in front of the Crimson Vault and hugged her knees to her chest in dismay and, dare she say it, fear. Reba Jean had the misty tendrils all woven together in a chain mail network in the ceiling, but neither of them had thought about the floor of the library! Seeping up through the floor was a roily mass of putrification that could have only come from the living room! She saw all sorts of rat-like varmints in the dark ooze as it churned across the floor like a flooded river. Where was Reba Jean? Had she already drowned in this maelstrom from within? Lady Jane was not sure how to proceed; she was not really in charge, but what of the treasures, was she not supposed to protect them with her life?

Hearing a whine, she looked down to see the little puppy jumping to get up with her on the table. Why was the puppy in the library? She snatched it up from the raging current and cuddled it on her lap. It grumbled and then settled down on her lap as she searched around for options. It yipped and whined as if to say it, too, was not content with its circumstances. Begging to be put down, it jumped from her lap and disappeared into Sir Theo's library, fussing at him. Oh no, was this black river of ratty ooze going to seep into Sir Theo's library too?

Reba Jean was under the impression that the library was secure. She felt like this issue was just centered in the living room, and even though it seemed to be seeping out onto those around her, she wasn't convinced that it was out of control. She again felt frustration with herself and everything around her. But why? Aha! It was a sign of discontentment, or at least, that is what she surmised. Reba Jean concentrated and tried to analyze why she was not content with her life. She knew again that it was because she felt like she was having to be the burden bearer of burdens that she did not want or think she should bear.

Jumping up from her seat in a frustrated huff, she went to the kitchen to get a brownie. In her thoughts though, she was mentally stomping around like a toddler having a tantrum. As she tidied up the kitchen from lunch, served herself a brownie, and pondered her lack of contentment, a little voice reminded her that she had not been in the prayer closet yesterday or today. She recalled her devotions just that morning about the priests and Levites who had not sufficiently sanctified themselves to perform the holy duties that they were called to do in the House of the Lord. She had related it to pastors and ministers of this current age, but here she was also of a holy, royal priesthood according to Scripture, and she was not cleansed or sufficiently sanctified.

Her ego, and thus her pride, was getting in the way; she needed to humble herself before the Lord and ask for His forgiveness and healing. Taking large bites of brownie, she knew it was time to head to the prayer closet. Why did she feel like she was going to the proverbial woodshed? Part of her was anxious to go spend time in prayer, but another part of her just wanted to sit, soak, sulk, and sour. A pity party seemed to have extended its invitation to her, and she had accepted and attended without even realizing it fully. The puppy was whiny and probably wanted a nap, yet there it went scurrying around the house with a toy rat. That rat reminded her of a lecture she had given months ago instructing that group of young librarians to be careful not to let rats into the library. OH MY! She thought of the acrostic she had used with the letters that spelled out R-A-T-S and realized she had rats right there in her own living room! The letter R stood for Rebellion and Resentment, the A was for Attitude, which was a by-product of anger, the T was for Temptation, and S was for Selfishness. The thought was as sharp as the acid that rose to her throat and the bite of the puppy's teeth as it tried to get her attention. It was way past time for Reba Jean to get into her prayer closet. She had rats trying to devour everything in the living room. If she wasn't careful, they would find their way into the library of treasures!

With a determined air, she strode outside and sat on the swing. She eyed a green dragonfly that settled down on a blade of green grass, trying to hide itself. She was reminded of the dragonfly that Mr. Insidious had changed her butterfly into a couple of months prior. She felt like this dragonfly was the same one. She eyed the yellowed, wilted, drying leaves of her squash plants and felt the spiritual comparisons on full display for her to apply to her own life. Bowing her head, she begged God to forgive her for her pride and resentment. Resentment, she was reminded, was not fully trusting in God for her life, so she was resenting everything going on because of her lack of trust.

Reba Jean finished praying, and wilting in the heat herself, she re-entered the cool air of the house and felt a resolve to stop being so rat infested. Prayer and trust would exterminate those rats that had invaded and, for a time, had taken over, wreaking ruin on all they could chew on. Reba Jean rubbed her cheek, and it reminded her of Lady Jane's scarred visage from a fierce battle in the library from much the same issues. Narrowing her eyes, she had an overwhelming urge to visit the library and check on Lady Jane.

Opening the door was not as easy as it used to be; there seemed to be something clogging the hinges. With a breathed prayer, Reba Jean shoved against the door with all her might and managed to squeeze into the narrow opening, barking her hip and shin on the doorframe. The stench was foul, and there were remnants of black ooze and rat excrement all over the floor. Aghast at the sight and smell, she picked up her skirt, and then realizing it was already befouled, she waded through the remnants of what looked like a river that had thrown up every piece of junk from the beginning of the world. This was vile!

"Lady Jane?" her voice shook as she called for her friend. A weak warbling response could be heard from further down the corridor. Reba Jean found the broken end of a bookshelf and using it like a battering ram, she shoved a clear path toward the source of the piteous cry. With heroic effort and all her strength nearly expended in the attempt, she found Lady Jane on the old, rugged table next to the oil lamp. With a heave, Reba Jean hoisted herself onto the table, and the two women collapsed into each other's arms and began to cry.

"Lady Jane, I am so sorry," began Reba Jean. "I truly believed you would be protected from the rest of the house since we fortified the library."

"Reba Jean, my dear, I also did not anticipate any issues from the living room! I feared for your life!" gasped Lady Jane in return. Exhausted and overwhelmed by the thought of yet another cleanup that would need to be done, they sat there on the table and soon fell into a fitful slumber.

Chapter 8

Reba Jean and Lady Jane worked on the massive cleanup of rodents and ooze that saturated the library's floor. Buckets of water from the fountain in the atrium did a thorough job of cleansing and sanitizing the floors. Hours later, they surveyed the results together, relieved that there did not seem to be any permanent damage since the infestation had not been there for any amount of time. Reba Jean left Lady Jane to rest and returned to the living room to decide on a course of action that would rid the house of all rats lurking about. She also needed to get a handle on the entire situation that made her feel like she had no control. With a determined air and some resignation, she decided to trust God for the future. If He decided to let her deal with the muddle her mouth had gotten into, then she needed to do it to the best of her ability and trust God to give her the strength to proceed. She looked up a few videos to help her with the added responsibility that she would shoulder in the next month. It left her almost anticipating the prospect instead of dreading it. The sleep she had gotten the last two weeks had also really helped. The time off work had also helped her body regain some of its strength.

Spying some flies in the kitchen, she was reminded that she needed to keep the house cleaner, somehow. Swatting the flies turned into a comedy of errors, with ripening tomatoes falling, bric-a-brac dropping, and smears of fly carcasses all over the windows. She laughed when she thought that Sunshine probably would not appreciate the spiritual applications that she could draw from fly carcasses.

Over the next couple of weeks, the library no longer felt safe to Lady Jane. She hated that the stillness was not holy; in fact, it amplified every sound including the sound of rats' claws skittering around. Oh, she had seen those red beady eyes on many occasions and heard their teeth gnawing on the floor and even on the books and strong boxes. Like years before, Lady Jane felt fear and anger at Reba Jean for not fortifying the library or the living room! She trounced down a corridor and saw a scroll on the wall talking about Being Still... Well, it sure was still in here, but she laughed scornfully, this was NOT a place that Lord Rabboni would be eager to visit. Feeling like she was being watched, she slanted her eyes sideways and saw an exceptionally large rat creature eyeing her, then with a lurch it started towards her. She shrieked and began to run, and as she did the rat seemed to grow larger with every step. This anger combined with her fears seemed to just spur the rat onward to its quarry, HER!

Where was Reba Jean? Where did Goodness and Mercy disappear to? Running through the aisles shrieking, she felt nibbles at her feet and ankles as the large rat seemed to multiply spontaneously into a horde of little rats. It was a losing battle, thought Lady Jane, and there would be no one to save her! All the holy artifacts and collected treasure did not seem to have any power in here anymore, she thought as she raced around in circles and up staircases and through dusty corridors, running for her very life. The bites she incurred welted up instantly and festered with putrefying soreness. She itched and scratched, tears streaming down her scarred cheeks, until she spotted a hidden crack in the wall. With a burst of sheer willpower, she slid into the crack into hot stifling darkness and hoped the rats couldn't smell her location.

Reba Jean had not written in her book or even visited the library for a few weeks. She had gone round and round with daily resentment and discontentment. Some days she fought the old, wicked thoughts, other days it was the new burden of responsibility. The recurring theme of "Be Still and Know that He is God" had been expanded to include Isaiah 40:31. Be still meant to also wait on the Lord, and He would RENEW her strength. Too many days though, the battles left her feeling like she needed a frontal lobotomy. She had often felt overcome of evil. Discouragement frequently reigned over her spirit, she knew it was resentment's companion, but nonetheless, knowing was only half the battle.

Still feeling the mistaken sense of security, she felt like the battle was only taking place in the living room. Surely, the library was fine; she had cleaned up after the last battle up there, thinking that the rats were gone. However, she had done NOTHING to fortify the floor of the library, or even given Lady Jane the ability to wield the Golden Sword in defense of herself. Surely Goodness and Mercy were following her around up there, she was probably much safer in the library than Reba Jean was down here in the Living Room.

The thoughts of treasures and the search for good thoughts no longer seemed important as they once had. The prayer closet was, of course, not in use, and even the other places of prayer were often interrupted by life's distractions. Reba Jean was barely surviving; she was most definitely not thriving.

Sitting down weeks later to finally write in her book, she had almost thought she would never even finish that. Her husband was going through his own issues of defeat as well, so it just felt so troubling and turbulent.

Then she received word that her first book might be printed in the next couple of weeks, and this felt like a boon to her spirit. Her husband almost acted disbelieving that she could produce anything worth publishing. The upcoming visit with her family he had labeled a "misfit convention" She had tried to laugh at that, but inwardly, it hurt. Yes, she was a misfit, she always had been. And her family was definitely dysfunctional. Again, she tried to reassure herself that God knew what He was doing when He had chosen this particular family for her to be born into. She wanted to grab her hair and rip it out in sheer frustration, though.

Closing her eyes, she felt as if she was out on the ocean heaving in a boat upon turbulent waters. The sensation of the waves was making her seasick, and she curled up into a ball on the bottom of the ship and tried not to cry. Feeling like she was going to be shipwrecked and drowned, she struggled to the side of the boat and feebly called for help. Looming out of the darkness a huge ship with guns and cannons forged across the waves and smashed her little vessel into smithereens. Drowning in the salty ocean that was even saltier than her tears, she felt a rough rope settle down over her torso and lassoed her tightly and painfully.

With an upward jerking motion, she was hoisted onto the deck of the ship, and squinting through tear-swollen eyes, she was surprised to see a tall, sinister pirate sneering at her in contempt!

"WELL, my pretty little wench, you serve me now!" he cackled maliciously.

Reba Jean quaked as she recognized the visage that peered at her luridly. It was Mr. Insidious, but he was now Captain Insidious! She was his prisoner on the Sea of Despair! Wait! How did she get into the ocean? She had been in her living room! Struggling and twisting in the ropes around her only made them cut into her soft skin even more. If she was very still, then they weren't as uncomfortable. However, the very thought of being comfortable in bondage was appalling. If she could just open her eyes, maybe it was just a nightmare. She closed her eyes tightly and counted "One-two-three-four..." towards Captain Insidious.

Captain Insidious eagerly rubbed his clawed hands together as he gleefully anticipated the next few minutes. Springing towards her, he violently slapped her on the cheek leaving long scratches from his claws. She felt her blood run down her cheek as her head snapped back and forth from the force of the slap. Black ooze from his claws burned into her skin, and she almost felt as if she deserved this torture at his hands. She felt sharp bites and nips at her ankles and realized the ship was infested with rats. Looking around, she noticed books from her library shelves and some strong boxes that had been in her library as well. What on earth! Was she on a ship, or was she in her library? Confusion and pain added to her disorientation. Was this still a nightmare, maybe from the sleeping potion she still had to take every night?

Blurry eyed, Reba Jean tried to see through the haze of blood and black ooze, almost making out what looked like another woman bound in ropes just like her a few yards away. If she was not mistaken, it surely looked as if Lady Jane was captive on this ship, too! Oddly resigned to this, and almost numb from the pain of the whole ordeal, Reba Jean just assumed she was beyond help. Captain Insidious had won, the rats would feast on her carcass, and she would die right here on the Sea of Despair. Captain Insidious shooed off some rats and chameleons that were harassing his prizes. With an unholy look in his beady eyes, he welcomed her and Lady Jane to the pirate ship aptly named the Flying Fiery Dart.

Lady Jane had thought she was hidden from the rats in that crevice in the wall, but the next thing she knew the floor was rolling under her feet and she was bound tightly in rough strong ropes. Rats scurried around her, and creepy chameleons climbed her skirts and pulled her hair. Petrified of where she had escaped to, she looked around. In front of her was a huge pirate gloating over another prisoner in front of him. Listening carefully, she collapsed inwardly as she recognized the sinister voice of Insidious! As he turned, she saw his captured prey was none other than her mistress, Reba Jean!

Reba Jean closed her eyes in disbelief, and as her thoughts swirled, she began to laugh as one who was out of their mind. Hysterically she said, "Inconceivable!" Pirates, rats of unusual size, this was just her tired brain manufacturing a version of a classic tale. She needed more sleep, she was not a prisoner on the Flying Fiery Dart, and Lady Jane was still safely secured in the serenity of the library. Still laughing hysterically, she was brought up short when another excruciating slap landed on her other cheek. Hearing a hiss near her ear, as her eyes were swollen shut, she felt her spirit completely drown within her as she heard Captain Insidious remind her in that unholy whisper that she was beyond help in his realm.

Reba Jean fell into a pain-induced stupor and had no strength to even fight against the bonds that bound her in their relentless grasp. She never felt them throw her into the dungeon or realize that she was even alive. She was locked inside an unconscious state almost as a means of mental self-preservation. Lady Jane was now at the mercy of Captain Insidious, and there did not seem to be any rescue in sight. Lady Jane felt herself grow desperate; she had never been out of the library before. The banished and forbidden books and strongboxes from the library were now on board the Fiery Dart. She watched the rats chewing on them and remembered how they had chewed on the good books and artifacts in the library.

Where were the Overseer, Lord Rabboni, and King Abba? How she longed for the golden swords to cut away her bonds. Lady Jane closed her eyes and tried to remember the Ancient One from the library. She had remembered a couple of words, but they could not seem to come into focus. Shivering violently, she struggled against her bonds. She had to find a way to save her mistress and herself from Captain Insidious and his vermin-infested pirate ship. She remembered the story of the apostles who sang in prison. "Rescue the perishing, care for the dying..." sprang to her mind; oh, that was not the context of the actual song, but it sure did apply to her current situation.

Captain Insidious turned to Lady Jane; she was starting to have that sickening sweet aroma that he despised. Somehow, she was trying to pray or praise the King of Heaven, even while she was in bondage on his ship! He needed to put an end to that immediately. With fierce strides, he was at her side, bellowing abominations at her. Lady Jane remembered something from one of Reba Jean's recent lectures. She had emphatically instructed that you can have selective hearing when it came to the noise from outside the library. You could just ignore it and not listen to it. She decided that as she was the avatar of the library, she could choose what she was going to listen to. She shut her ears against the sewage spilling out of the pirate's mouth and dug down into her memory of good things from the Ancient One. Ah yes, there it was, the verse that said: "...pray for them which despitefully use you and persecute you." Oh! What would happen if she prayed for Captain Insidious?

That thought was so, well, so inconceivable! He was a demon, not a person, but she could pray that his attacks would not succeed! It would be easier if Reba Jean was praying with her, but maybe she needed to pray for Reba Jean too! Then the thought grew stronger; yes, prayer was indeed her secret weapon. A mosquito bit her on her leg, the rats swarmed her, and the other creatures descended on her as she began to pray to King Abba. She shivered and almost gave up; the pain was unbearable. She squirmed and contorted in her bonds. Captain Insidious flicked his whip, and it lashed her skin with torturous stripes. He was most intent on keeping her from praying, and he would not let his ship be overrun by a little strip of a girl.

Reba Jean awoke from her self-induced coma only to realize she was still in bondage. Her living room and the library were nowhere in sight, the waves nauseated her, and she could feel every wound and nick on her body. Okay, so she was here; now what? She took mental soundings of her surroundings, as her eyes were still too swollen to see anything clearly in this dark, dank dungeon. How did she get here? She needed to leave; she had a lecture to prepare for on Monday, a meeting for VBS tomorrow, and a book to write! She needed to get out of this dungeon and back to her own life! "Be still and KNOW that I am God..." rang in her mind. Ok, be still, was step one, wait on the Lord, was step two. She stilled her pain-wracked body and tortured mind and forced herself to concentrate on the Lord. It seemed to take a herculean effort to stop thinking about all the things that had transpired in the last few weeks, the memories that had risen to the surface, and the uncertainty that was prevalent. She realized that this is what had brought her to the dungeon she was now ensnared within.

Lady Jane sensed that Reba Jean was conscious again, and she could feel the fluttering of hope in her chest as she continued to pray for her mistress. She kept her eyes closed so that she could not see what Captain Insidious was doing or be distracted by his villainous vermin. Her heart cried out to King Abba and Lord Rabboni on behalf of Reba Jean. She was aware that the answer and help may not be immediate. She was even conscious of the story that Daniel of old had to wait twenty-one days for help to arrive. Well, she purposed, if Daniel could wait and pray for twenty-one long days, then surely, she could too.

Captain Insidious saw a particular expression settle upon Lady Jane's features that had him fuming. She thought she could pray herself out of this situation, and her resoluteness only fueled his determination to inflict as much torture on her as he could imagine. He cracked his whip, and his minions scurried to attention while Lady Jane flinched at the sound. With a harsh cackle, he assembled his crew to prepare for the long voyage ahead. A chameleon perched itself on his shoulder, and he scratched its head with pride as he pondered what to do now that he had his prey firmly within his grasp. Aha! He would send ransom demands to the King on the slight chance that He wanted these worthless wenches back into His family. Yes! By all that was unholy, this was the perfect plan.

Reba Jean kept her focus on the Lord, and soon, it was almost as if she could hear a melody ringing in her heart. Words from various worship songs began to chime through the chambers of her heart. "It Is No Secret What God Can Do," "And He Walks and Talks with Me," and "It Is Well With My Soul" all played through in a secret symphony. She remembered that she was a child of the King of Heaven; He would be with her and never forsake her even when she got herself into trouble like she was even now. *It is no secret what God can do, what He had done for others, He would do for her*, she ran the next few lines through her mind and realized that His pardon would free her. Reba Jean slumped to the foul, wretched-smelling floor of the dungeon and humbly asked God to once again forgive her for not walking with Him as closely as she should. She also asked Him to pardon her and ransom her from the clutches of Captain Insidious and the dreaded Sea of Despair.

Captain Insidious plucked his pet dragonfly from its cage near the mainsail, and, penning a ransom note in a hurried manner, he attached it to the winged varmint and cast it aloft to carry it to the celestial realm. The ransom note read, "The wenches of the library are now within my control; you may have them in exchange for the deed to the library." Restlessly, he awaited any reply from the celestial realm. He was so full of himself that he actually thought he could make a deal with the King of Kings! That stupid dragonfly had better not get eaten by some eagle before it even got the ransom note to the other world. Belatedly, he realized that he perhaps should have sent an escort guard with that winged courier. With a swipe of his whip, he dispatched minions of armed guards to catch up with the dragonfly to ensure that the ransom note made its diabolical way to its destination.

The dragonfly did indeed make it to the gates of the celestial realm, where it was immediately detained along with its escort. The note found its way to the throne room of the Almighty. He had already been aware of the ongoing siege of the library and its residents. He was not unfeeling or uncaring to the needs of even His weakest children. Reba Jean's and Lady Jane's prayers had wafted upward to the altar of incense, and their sweet savor had mingled with the millions of others.

King Abba and Lord Rabboni had already sent a battalion of angelic ministers to the poor souls begging for help. King Abba blew on the dragonfly, and with that powerful burst of holy breath, the dragonfly was freed of its previous master's evil mechanisms and found itself flitting through a lovely garden in a hidden glade undiscovered by the Nether World. The minions were thrust straight to the gates of the Nether Realm, where they fell upon each other with a vengeance blaming each other for their capture and banishment.

Reba Jean felt the melody ringing in her heart and the verses running through her mind giving her strength. She pulled herself upright and felt the bonds loosen from their constricting grip around her. A bit surprised, she squirmed and twisted, and with a few agonizing contortions, she shrugged the bonds off her. Now, just to figure out how to get out of this dark, dank dungeon. With the thoughts of the apostles singing and the people praying in the stories of old, she continued her singing and praying. Oh, she knew it wasn't her voice that would be key, but her humble heart and her trust in the Lord that would free her even if just mentally or emotionally.

Chapter 9

A mighty crack thundered from stern to aft of the ship as it rammed into some immovable force in the Sea of Despair. With a heaving shudder, the Flying Fiery Dart began to crumble and crack. Captain Insidious bellowed and stormed at the crew, lashing his whip and hurling commands that went unheeded as the mighty ship began to sink. Lady Jane and Reba Jean felt their bodies lifted from this ship by an unseen force. They were being rescued, not just ransomed! A few brief moments of flashing lights and wisps of clouds, and then they were transported right back into the library.

Goodness and Mercy appeared as if out of nowhere and ministered to their wounds with the balm from Gilead, oil, and living water from the fountain. Reba Jean and Lady Jane collapsed into each other's arms mentally communicating all that they had endured, as words seemed to fail them. Suddenly, they both seemed to come to their senses and knelt on the floor of the library, thanking King Abba for rescuing them, and helping them even when they had surely failed Him.

A whisper of pages turning beckoned them to the Ancient One; King Abba had a message for them. Matthew 6:19-34 was highlighted in brilliant, iridescent gold. Together they carefully read the passage. There was so much in here to meditate and apply. Reba Jean reached towards a bookshelf and found a book with blank pages inside. She began to take notes on this passage of Scripture, about treasure, light, thieves, masters, and seekers. Lady Jane pondered what she was reading in this Ancient Book of books. She looked at the verse about serving two masters, and this really seemed to strike a chord in her. She served Reba Jean and Insidious but claimed to belong to King Abba. She needed to be single-minded, literally loyal to one Master, King Abba.

Captain Insidious choked on the salty water as he found himself drowning in his own sea. With a scream of rage, he hurled himself downward, breaking through the veil between worlds. Landing in Nether Realm he lashed his whip at everything around him and stormed his way upwards towards the library. He had lost his hostages, and the library was still under the protection of the Holy King. With evil rage, he began banging on the door of the library, creating a horrendous racket. Spotting some of his rat brigade, he screeched commands for them to find those cracks from before and chew their way into the library. He commanded them to make a hole big enough in the floor this time for himself to be able to gain entrance.

He had forgotten that he had been banished forever from the library; he was so enraged that he just assumed he could break his way in again. Filled with hate, he kept up a relentless violent pounding on the door of the library. He would break down this door, and if those women were within as he suspected, he would torture them until they begged for death. He had often encouraged them to kill themselves or kill others, this time he would oppress them so much that they would follow through with the unholy deed.

The women heard the thunderous pounding on the door, but within the library, it just sounded like muffled thuds that could be anything from Sir Theo to the crazy zoo. However, just to be safe, Reba Jean took strands of golden dust motes and designed a beautiful strong inner door which she installed in front of the original door. Then as she heard chewing sounds coming from the floorboards, she ran to the fountain and began splashing water all over the floor drowning the rats that were trying to chew their way into the library. The chewing sounds stopped; the muffled thuds were ignored with selective hearing. But, how was she going to get back to the living room? Was she now a prisoner in the library? That sounded like a happy fate with Lady Jane and the library's current spiritual condition.

With the Golden Sword, she carefully cut a secret hatch into the library wall and dug a tunnel down to the living room. This took more time than it seemed, and she was very concerned that someone would discover the secret entrance. With that thought in mind, she covered each entrance with a crimson tapestry. After a lot of work, both in the library and the living room, she felt as if progress had been achieved. Hugging Lady Jane tightly and thankfully, she left her sweet avatar in the contented confines of the library. Hiding the entrance to the library, she took stock of what was going on in the living room and the rest of the house while she had been lost at sea.

Oddly enough, things seemed to be the same as they had been when she had closed her eyes what seemed like days ago. The zoo was still clamoring for attention, her husband was doing his thing in his office as usual, and life seemed to be going on without any sign of pirates or rats. Was she the same, or was she different? Reba Jean took mental and spiritual stock of herself. Picking up her Bible from the dining room table she read again that passage in the book of Matthew. Verses nineteen through twenty-two leaped off the page at her, "Lay not up for yourselves treasures upon earth, where moth and rust doth corrupt, and where thieves break through and steal: But lay up for yourselves treasures in heaven, where neither moth nor rust doth corrupt, and where thieves do not break through nor steal: For where your treasure is, there will your heart be also."

She knew that someone or something was robbing her of her joy, and her mind seemed always to be corrupt. She had been assaulted by pirates and rats; she had not even thought about moths or rust! She had kept an eye out for chameleons and dragonflies, but moths?! Looking around the kitchen, she saw flies and bugs, but no moths. She would not be surprised to find them, however, as it seemed like her house was inundated with insectoid vermin.

Oddly, she slept well, and her dreams were nearly forgettable that night. The next day, however, she felt numb; there was a lot on her mind including the lecture she was to give the next day. She had run different topics through her mind, thought of past lectures, prayed, and asked the Lord what He would have her say, but no clarity yet. She sorely wanted to take a nap but felt a restlessness in her spirit. Was the library secure? Were the treasures she had collected even there, or had they been robbed while she was held hostage on that pirate ship?

With trepidation, she acted as casually as she could around the house until she saw a moment to slip behind that crimson tapestry and climb the tunnel up to the secret hatch in the library. Slipping into the cool confines of the library, Reba Jean sucked in a breath or two, then let her eyes adjust to the change of lighting. Straining her ears, she heard only the babbling of the fountain and not the sweet music from the other chamber. Gulping, she hurried to the music chamber and saw all the notes and lyrics just paused in mid-air. Panicking, she looked around to see how to restart the music of praise to the King. If it had been in the living room, she would have hit a button on the remote. Was this a signal that she had truly been robbed of her joy? Wait, no, it was here; it just wasn't working. Aha, that was the problem. She had joy; she was, however, not letting it be her strength! She wasn't allowing it to work in her life!

Tears running down her face, she sank to the floor in a defeated heap. She really had no words, so she let her heart cry out to her Heavenly Father to help the music start again. The silence was not comforting, but neither was it foreboding, it just did not seem appropriate. She waited and could faintly hear the orchestrated music from the living room down below. She strained with her heart to make out the lyrics. She was sure she knew the words, but they didn't seem to form clearly in her mind. Concentrating as hard as she could, she could feel the music seeping into her soul even if the words were not clear. Soon the music seemed louder, and she suddenly realized that she had pulled it up out of the living room and into the library. Peeking through her tear-laden eyes, she saw the golden notes streaming through the air, but the lyrics were still stuck in place. Maybe Captain Insidious had slapped her so hard that her brain couldn't remember the words? Well, at least she had the music playing again, maybe the words would come later.

Meandering out of the music room, she took an inventory of the artifacts to make sure they were in their proper places. Glancing up at the chainmail link canopy she looked for rusty links; she would need to treat them with oil if there were any. The sweet sound of Blessed Assurance wafted through the air, and she started crying as she realized she knew the words to this one. Standing in the middle of the atrium, she closed her eyes and sang along with her heart. She knew the lyrics were now wafting their way upward to the celestial realm and cascading like waterfalls of praise.

Lady Jane heard the beautiful praise music and let it draw her to the atrium, where she joined Reba Jean, and with clasped hands they worshipped King Abba and Lord Rabboni. The perfect song, as always, seemed to play just when they needed it. *Blessed Assurance, oh what a foretaste of glory divine, perfect submission...all is at rest.* Grateful hearts and hands were raised in thankful praise in the middle of the library that afternoon. Then, as happens with human frailty, the horrors of the day before, and the peace of the moment caught up with them, and they collapsed upon the settee and fell asleep.

While the women were at rest, there was no rest for the wicked. Captain Insidious howled in fury as an avalanche of drowned rats rained down upon his head. His hostages had been rescued, he had been shipwrecked, his pet dragonfly had completely disappeared, and his crew and army were all attacking each other instead of the enemy. Boiling with rage, he cracked his whip and lashed out at any minion close enough to reach with that cat of nine tails. Viciously, he whipped his scurvy army into a large group of skulking, disgruntled foot soldiers. Captain Insidious commanded them to stay put until he could conjure up a new strategy to employ.

Stomping away from the door of the library, he descended to a dark cavern he often resorted to and began to run scenarios through his head. He was struck by the oddity of his get-up, and the whole pirate ship scenario made him pause. Pirates were notorious for evil deeds, but usually for robbing other ships and places of value. What were Reba Jean and Lady Jane hiding? Pirates hid treasure, usually something they had looted from others. Did Lady Jane and Reba Jean somehow have a treasure they were hiding in the library? What could those two possibly have acquired that held any significance or value? He was sure it wasn't money, and the only gold in there was that celestial stuff that burned when it touched him. His eyes squeezed into a vicious slant as he figured he would have to go on a treasure hunt of his own. Somehow, they had managed to fortify the roof, walls, and doors of the library into a near impregnable fortress. The floors seemed to still be accessible or had been if the rats had done enough damage before they were washed away. The only way into the library was through the floor, and that could only be accessed through the living room! Aha!

Captain Insidious grabbed his team leaders and assembled them to discuss a new strategy, an attack on the living room! The living room and library were intricately linked together, so an attack on one was an attack on both. It was soon clear however, that no one seemed to know what the living room looked like or had even been there. They had concentrated so much on the library that the living room was unexplored. Word was sent far and wide in search of any minion who might know how to attack the living room.

A few other captains heard of his inquiry and joined in the strategy sessions. It seemed difficult to attack the living room of a ransomed child of the Celestial King. The library was easier to attack, but the living room was where the Overseer resided. They were no match for the Overseer no matter how strong and many they were when banded together. Surely, there was a way to at least sneak in a scout to gather information. Captain Insidious thought of his chameleon crew, they might be just the ticket. They would appear to be spiritual kinfolk and could gather intel on the best way to get victory without the Overseer interfering. The captains conferred, and all agreed that new chameleon scouts needed to be dispatched as Reba Jean seemed to have already discovered the last ones and their true intentions.

Chapter 10

Reba Jean and Lady Jane awoke within seconds of each other, stretching lazily as the music flowed over them peacefully. It reminded Reba Jean of an incident a few days prior when she had the beautiful hymn playing "Draw Me Nearer," in the living room and she headed to work and the CD in the car also began playing the same hymn, different style of music, same words. She had sung that song the rest of the day; she knew how valuable it was. Rolling over too far, she fell off the settee and landed with a soft thud and a giggle onto the library floor. Noticing the holes that the rats had chewed like a swarm of termites, she again pondered how to rebuild and re-enforce the floor. Casting about for an idea, her eyes caught Lady Jane's, and together they looked for something to use that wasn't destructible.

Reba Jean's eyes grew rounder than pancakes when the lyrics of a song ran through her mind, standing on the promises of God's Word. Then the passage of Scripture about building your life on the rock and not on the sand raced in behind. "Lady Jane! We need to make a floor out of the Rock of Ages and tile it with the promises of God's Word," gushed Reba Jean. Running together to the Ancient One, they opened it to the verses about leading me to the rock that is higher than I.

"Okay, Reba Jean, now what?" questioned Lady Jane. "The misty tendrils used to do this, sometimes the golden dust motes, but how do we get the rocks from God's Word into the floor of the library?"

Reba Jean heard a verse run through her mind, *Thy word have I hid in mine heart, that I might not sin against Thee.* With a thought of wonderment, Reba Jean pondered and then finally voiced her thoughts. "Lady Jane, I have this odd feeling that I have to shore up the floor from the living room side." Beautiful wonders had always happened in the library, but the living room was where reality reigned. Was it possible that the verses of Scripture that she had hidden in the living room were the way to fortify the library from the outside? "Lady Jane, my dear, I need to return to the living room and figure out how to repair the floor with the tools I have hidden away down there. I am not sure how long this will take or even how to make it happen without misty tendrils and golden dust motes."

"Be strong in the Lord and in the power of His might, my dear. I shall see you once your task is finished," bid Lady Jane in farewell to her mistress.

Reba Jean returned to the living room and just seemed at a loss; she had no idea how to turn Scripture into solid rocks. Maybe she was going crazy, for real this time. It sounded all good up there in the library, but down here, in reality, it just did not seem possible. The chewed floor gnawed at her, figuratively, of course, but all the same. She glanced at the clock; she had a meeting to attend, and she had no idea what her lecture topic was going to be for the next day. The lovely, orchestrated music was still playing on the television, and her husband was very quiet and detached in his office. She probably had rocks in her head, and not in a good way.

Her sister had sent her a video yesterday that had changed the way she viewed things in her life. As she thought about the video, the song "I Need Thee, Every Hour" began to play, and she clung to that desperately. The video talked about signs and symptoms of a common disorder that in girls often goes undiagnosed for far too long. Her sister said she thought she had four of the five symptoms herself. Reba Jean was aware of that possibility and had been ever since she had deduced that her mother probably had this undiagnosed Syndrome. She often rebelled against being reared in such a dysfunctional family. However, this video brought to light that the very ways that she thought she was fighting against the inherited genes were, in fact, the very signals that she was afflicted. Her ways of coping were a result of trying to mask or hide and to appear normal and functioning. Reba Jean had all five of the symptoms that predicted that she had it too.

This answered so many questions, however, now it also meant there was no cure; there was just the continuing coping that she had learned to do all her life. Sadly, she had discussed this with her husband, who said not to believe everything you read on the internet. He assured her that he still loved her, but today he seemed detached and even withdrawn. He had always feared that she would become like her mother, and now she had basically told him that she was defective. What he didn't realize is that he also behaved with many of the same characteristics that her mother did. He probably had the Syndrome, too, but was sure to deny it. *Normal is highly overrated*, Reba Jean thought to herself.

The strains to "Take it to the Lord in Prayer" caressed her thoughts... we should never be discouraged... that was exactly how she had been feeling at that moment. The Heavenly Father knew what she was made of, He had allowed her to be this way. There was no healing on this side of Heaven, but He still chose to use her for His service. She felt she had a harder time than other people seemed to, and yet they probably never even realized how hard it was for her to do things or even cope. It made sense now why she did not like people or "people" very well. Her awkwardness and social skills were something she now had a label for.

She was still Reba Jean; having a diagnosis or even a myriad of questions finally answered did nothing to change who she was. She was just going to have to get a grip and not let this defeat her. Her sister said it was liberating to know. Reba Jean did not really agree, because she would not be able to tell anyone, much less use it as an excuse to fall apart and not cope as she had all these years. The beloved notes of her favorite hymn began to

71

play as if exactly on cue, "It is Well with my Soul". Yes, it was well with her soul, even if her mind and body were not always well. "Christ has regarded my helpless estate and has shed His own blood for my soul" rang through her melancholy thoughts. *Ok, suck it up Buttercup*, Reba Jean remonstrated herself.

It was time to pretend to be functioning and get ready for the meeting and then church afterwards. She had no clue what the lecture would be on tomorrow, but she had learned to just trust the Lord for the words when things like this happened. She hoped she hadn't somehow missed something He had tried to tell her. She didn't think so since she seemed to hear every encouragement, He sent her way today.

After church and its encouraging service, she confronted her husband about her so-called diagnosis. He told her in no uncertain terms that he did not know how her mother had managed to have four children with her issues, but there was no way that Reba Jean had the Syndrome regardless of what the internet said. He loved her, despite her issues. She was starting to reconcile that maybe she wasn't as damaged as she had thought she was. Her pastor had spoken of something in his message tonight that helped her understand how to fix the floor of the library. With that reminder of that very necessary task, she began quoting Scripture towards the living room ceiling. Psalm 18:30 "As for God, his way is perfect: the word of the Lord is tried: he is a buckler to all those that trust in him." The Word of the Lord is a buckler, a shield, a defense, that was a verse that could seep through the chewed floorboards of the library and fill them in. James 1:21 was directed upward next, "Wherefore lay apart all filthiness and superfluity of naughtiness, and receive with meekness the engrafted word, which is able to save your souls." How literal was that verse when applied to her situation? Psalm 107:20 seemed applicable, "He sent his word, and healed them, and delivered them from their destructions."

Reba Jean found multiple Scriptures that she read inwardly and knew they would help fill in the gaps in the floor. Matthew 7:24 took it a step further, "Therefore whosoever heareth these sayings of mine, and doeth them, I will liken him unto a wise man, which built his house upon a rock." It wasn't just hearing the Word; it was doing what God said in His Word. Her living room and library needed to be built upon a rock, the Rock of Ages. As she lay in bed that night, she began to believe that the lecture the next day would be canceled, yet just before she finally fell asleep hours later, a topic and Scripture passage came to mind.

Sure enough, the next morning, the lecture was canceled due to the arrival of the plague among the itinerant librarians. Reba Jean kept that passage of Scripture in mind as she went to work, however. Maybe it applied to her and her situation in the library. She returned home to further study the passage found in 2 Peter 1:3-12, things to add to her faith which was the foundation she was to build upon. Verse four jumped out with the words "exceeding great and precious promises" as well. Those words signified treasure in her mind. The promises of God were not to be used to physically stand upon like tiles on a floor as she had originally thought she might do. No, these promises were to be kept and valued as treasure.

Reba Jean mentally reviewed the treasures she was currently keeping in her library. She needed to shore up the foundation, fill in the cracks, and keep the library strong, established, and fortified. Importantly, it all needed to commence from the living room, the heart of the home. Just like Lady Jane was the avatar of the library, the library itself was just a reflection of what was really transpiring in the living room. She continued to read verses five through seven and pictured the characteristics of a godly life as stones being placed under the porous, rat-bitten floorboards of the library overhead.

73

Feeling confident that progress was being swiftly made to rectify the lapse in security, Reba Jean decided to lay down and rest before the start of Vacation Bible School that evening. She was a bit paranoid about closing her eyes, however. She had no desire to end up in some dungeon at the mercy of some demonic hoodlum again. Maybe she should go up to the library to rest, that might be safer. Casting her eyes in all directions to ensure no one was watching, she once again slid behind the crimson tapestry, climbed up the tunnel, and opened the hidden hatch. Feeling a scratching on her leg and something jumping on her, she muffled a shriek. With a sudden exhale of relief, she discovered the puppy had followed her scent into the library. The puppy followed her to the settee, and together they plopped down in hopes to rest in the tranquility of the sacred space. Lady Jane could be heard humming sweetly from the chamber of praise and seemed oblivious to their arrival. Ahh, surely, she could rest for a short time up here without pirates, rats, or nasty, nefarious, ne'er-do-wells interrupting.

The week of Vacation Bible School went extremely well, and so many precious young souls were saved from the eternal fires of hell, including one precious young girl that she had been praying for all these months. Her husband actually helped this year unsolicited and had amazingly kept his impatience in check. It almost seemed surreal! Reba Jean spent much time thanking the Lord for so many answered prayers.

She needed to focus on the treasures that somehow, with work and stress, had been slipping out of focus. She was still surprised when the mental suggestion to kill herself or someone else slipped into her mind. She would almost laugh out loud, the idea was so bizarre, life was so sacred. How did the forces of the Nether World think this could be a successful temptation? She had a feeling they were getting desperate. The abominable thoughts had pretty much subsided; she would ask forgiveness immediately the moment they tried to pass through her mental palace.

The other stressors, smaller in nature, still threatened to overwhelm her. She still wanted to downsize her zoo and eliminate the potential of the second job. However, that was postponed for at least another week or so. She was starting to sleep better, and that always helped her mental issues. Her husband, however, was getting on the socializing kick again, and that really was going to take a lot of fortitude and prayer to "people." Did other people have problems with social awkwardness without having a disorder?

Jerking to a start, she realized that she had been mentally stewing in the library! Looking around and peering fearfully at the chainmail network of misty tendrils, she feared she was about to create mayhem as had happened in time past in the library. The library used to be a very dangerous place to be in with wayward thoughts tramping through the aisles. Reba Jean realized she hadn't seen Lady Jane at all on this visit to her gilded cage. This bothered her as she did not hear the hymns playing; had Lady Jane been kidnapped, assaulted, taken prisoner by the dread, demon pirate gang?

Reba Jean felt her anxiety claw at her as she began racing through the library searching for Lady Jane. She did not dare call out, and she really had no reason for the unexplained fear that gripped her vocal cords. Racing up the stairs to the various levels, and frantically searching corridors and dimly lit corners, she found the crevice that had sucked Lady Jane into the Sea of Despair. Only now a brick wall blocked the portal to the underworld. The celestial companions were not visible, the artifacts were in their places, and it didn't appear that the library was under siege. Where was Lady Jane?

The usual places were empty, even Sir Theo's library was quiet except for the steady hum of his bees working away with their data storage. She did not seek answers from the Ancient One or use the oil Lamp to help her search. The golden Swords lay inert, the fountain only bubbled sporadically, and Lady Jane was just GONE! The puppy nosed around interested in its own treasure hunt and did not seem to realize that anything was amiss. Where was Lady Jane? If Lady Jane was gone, did that mean she had lost her mind?

Captain Insidious had assembled his drowned rats and sent them through the sulfuric lava pits, where the black ooze of the underworld would re-fortify them with rebellion, resentment, anger, temptation, etc. The tarry pits seared the wounds the living water had left on his rat brigade, and now he could dispatch them to other targets. Sitting with his military counsel, he pulled out the manual of how to rob a Christian. The manual stated that their testimony was the ultimate goal to tarnish and steal from them. "Ok, you scallywags, let's be the pirates that she thinks we are; it's time to go pillage and destroy!"

Armed with the knowledge from centuries of research, Captain Insidious knew that he had to attack and steal Reba Jean's sanity, security, surety, story, and steadfastness. He read all the "s" words and his hiss increased intensely. Oh, how he loved "S" words; they slithered off his tongue so deliciously. "How s-s-s-sati-s-s-s-fying, this quest would be" thought Captain Insidious. Glancing over at his chameleon company, he remembered that he still hadn't selected any new scouts. Were they a necessary asset right now?

The one scout he had used before sat dejected, nursing some unknown plague it had acquired from the upper world excursion.

The puppy got all frantic and demanding, scratching Reba Jean's legs as she frantically searched the library for Lady Jane. With frustration, she chased it into a chamber and shut it away from being underfoot. Her angst arose, and yet she still did not call for Lady Jane. Her voice just seemed paralyzed in her throat. If she vocalized her mounting terror, would it come to life? She had not started her day with reading the Bible like she knew she should; was this the reason that she felt like she was the one that was lost?

Should she just read some of the Ancient One, and then resume her search? Where were Goodness and Mercy? If they were following her, why couldn't she see them? In her haste, she barked her shin against a wooden strongbox jutting out into the aisle. That was going to leave a bruise, everything bruised her these days. Her panic seemed mixed with frustration and maybe even anger, where was Lady Jane?! Her facial expression became petulant, and she stood in the middle of an aisle of books that used to document every thought she ever had. Tapping her foot, she tried to decide if she was going to calm down and read Scripture or run pell-mell in endless circles looking for Lady Jane.

Halfway down a darkened aisle of books, she crossed her arms as goosebumps rose on her flesh causing her to shiver with cold, fear, and a myriad of emotions too many to list. She didn't want to look too closely at the titles of these books; surely the bad ones had been locked away, but this aisle seemed laced with pent-up emotions. Shivering even more, she tried to calm down, she did not want to cause bedlam with bad books. Titles seemed to glow orange, the dog whined, and she couldn't stop shivering. Reba Jean stopped in the middle of the aisle and found she could not make any sort of decision. To go, stay, read, run, or scream, none of these seemed even possible. Thoughts of her half-written book came to mind, none of her friends had finished reading it, the editor hadn't even stated she had finished it or liked it. The second book would probably be unfinished, or here would lie Reba Jean, lost in the library forever.

There were no physical restraints on her, yet she felt bound and imprisoned by something. Her husband could be heard in the kitchen, making his lunch, she felt almost guilty for not jumping in to help him, but she was stuck, in her own library. The puppy was getting frantic for being locked away, the yips only added to her increasing frustration. The smell of food made her hungry, but that only frustrated her; she was supposed to go out to dinner tonight, so she did not want to overeat. She had finally begun losing weight. Her head hurt, her stomach rumbled, and she shivered. Why did it seem like an insurmountable task just to read the Bible?

Frustratedly frowning, she managed to inch her way out of that particular aisle, and defeatedly released the puppy from its prison. Her goosebumps subsided a bit, but her head still ached. She looked at the Ancient One, and it seemed to lovingly beckon her to find solace and strength in Its pages. Where did this reluctance come from? She wanted help and hope; it was right there within her grasp, yet she held herself aloof. Then with almost a sob, Reba Jean lurched towards the Ancient One feeling like a paralyzed cripple and sank at the bottom of the pedestal inwardly crying. She still did not open its pages, and it did not open Itself for her.

Lady Jane was blissfully unaware of all that was going on in the library with Reba Jean. She had discovered a gallery of memories that she had nearly forgotten and had begun to explore some deep recesses of the library. With the fortifications in place, she felt secure that pulling out these memories and examining them would be harmless. Sir Theo had mentioned a few things the night before, and she wanted to see if they were in this gallery.

Trailing her fingers along dusty shelves, she peered at their contents and felt herself slip into a daydream. It was interesting to see how perspectives and perceptions varied from person to person. How she remembered things and the emotions they invoked were different than how say Sir Theo or Mister Jimothy remembered them.

The puppy found her and begged to be held. Without thinking, Lady Jane cuddled the puppy, which seemed to be in the library more often than ever. Was it possible that it came up here without help? Squirming to get down, it seemed to beg her to follow it. Lady Jane amusedly followed the puppy and soon they found themselves inside a lovely portico that she had not known existed. She entered a lovely scene with a rug, rocking chairs, and even a bench swing. A lovely breeze made the whole sunny room comfortable. Hummingbirds could be seen flitting around, and the puppy joined a large dog on the rug. Oh, this was an even better spot to daydream, thought Lady Jane.

Long, blissful moments of peaceful silence ensued, until the puppy started barking, the large dog got frantic, and the breeze turned to humid heat. She restlessly followed the barking puppy back into the library, wondering what was causing such a stir with the puppy. It scampered around barking, until she finally remonstrated it with, "Be quiet. You'll wake up the books!" She wandered back to her boudoir, with the puppy fussing quietly at her side. Fastening her eyes on her bedside table she saw a clutter of stuff, but then shrugged; she did not feel like cleaning today. Clutter wasn't dangerous, was it? Lady Jane shivered and watched goosebumps rise on her arms; hmmm, something was just not right in the library.

Reba Jean just wanted to sit and sob; she had a feeling it was all the emotions and exhaustion causing this melt-down. She brushed her hair out of her face and knew she would need a shorter hairstyle. Her stomach rumbled again, and she wondered if she should eat something. Going to the kitchen would get her out of this library, maybe that would be safer than up here where the walls seemed to be closing in on her. She still wondered why she couldn't just sit down and read Scripture, but this had happened multiple times before until she just made herself do it. Her guilt complex was revving into overdrive. One moment she was praising the Lord for souls saved, and a good week, and the next moment she was fighting a battle of wills about reading Scripture. It almost seemed laughable when you put it as simply as that. A battle of wills. Then a thought came to her mind. What if she was supposed to read something that would help her, and the forces of evil did NOT want her to read it? Something that would help her find treasure? Her eyes grew big, and her determination inserted itself, she was going to read Scripture, and read it right now!

The puppy settled down for a nap by itself (that was a miracle) as she opened Scripture. She had been studying the Book of Leviticus. There was so much to learn and draw parallels to her own Christian life held within this book of priestly ordinances of old. This chapter was all about God telling His people that "I am the LORD your God!" It also touched on all the abominations to abhor, and she felt the stern reminder to not even think of the abominations. That shored it up in her mind, those thoughts just had to be completely shut down. It went even further than resisting, her mind needed to be an impenetrable fortress. She meditated on the seriousness of being set apart and usable for the Lord's service. Sanctification and purification were vital, maybe these, too, were part of the treasure trove that she was hunting.

Her stomach rumbled, and she knew with dinner plans still unsettled that she needed to at least nibble on something. She did not want to disturb the sleeping puppy; she was just happy it did not need to be held for once. With that observation, she bowed her head and once again asked the Lord to help her with the zoo and the upcoming stressors that seemed to overwhelm her more than necessary. As she prayed, a cat came over to seek attention; was it possible that the underworld was trying to distract her time in the Throne Room? She wanted to scream, just some uninterrupted time without the zoo, obligations, people… She felt hot acid rise up in her throat; she had made the mistake of bowing her head. So many times, she did better if she acted like she wasn't praying at all. Sure enough, the cat wandered off, and she could continue praying if she did not look like she was.

Calming down because she did not want to pray in anger, she once again tried to speak with her Creator and not at Him. Sure enough, the cat came back and sank its claws into her leg. Frustrated, she stood up and ignored the barking of the big dog and looked for some place she could lock herself away in to pray and be alone with the Lord. This was so frustrating it was almost laughable. She found herself outside on the swing, and oddly enough, the dogs were calm and quiet while she prayed. That did not last as long as she had hoped, and once again, frustration set in. She wandered back inside, still thinking she should eat something. The zoo was frustrating her, and she found herself restless. Again, she silently pleaded with the Lord to intervene with the zoo and her stress.

She had housework to do. Her husband had helped by doing some already this morning, but she was just plain worn out. The expression 'worn to a frazzle' seemed very applicable. She forgot that Lady Jane was missing, and she even forgot to guard her mind. She just wanted to immerse herself in some sort of mind-numbing activity, blocking out all the stress. With resignation, she started to do housework while trying to figure out what would work for lunch. The dogs were still restless and seeking attention, and she just wanted to run away.

The housework felt monumental, but she stabbed away at it anyway, trying half-heartedly not to be resentful of the never-ending laundry and dishes and dirty floors. She baked lunch in the oven, regretting her decision, sure that she would end up putting back on the weight she had fought so hard to lose this last week. The puppy whined just as discontentedly as she felt. Her only recourse, it seemed, was to sit on the couch and drown her thoughts in a television show and pizza. The thought of this made her curl her lips in disgusted frustration. What she wouldn't give for a good book to read, besides her own half-written meanderings.

A few days went by with their usual issues; nothing had really changed. The thought of killing herself or others really bothered her. Why did the devil think that was something she could be tempted to do? It baffled her to think that such a suggestion would even come to mind on so many various occasions. Then it was as if the Holy Spirit illuminated the mystery by reminding her that Satan had even tempted Jesus to kill Himself. This wasn't anything new, and mercy me, he even thought he could get Jesus to kill himself?! She read Matthew 4:1-11 just to make sure she was correct. Verses five and six stated, "Then the devil taketh him up into the holy city, and setteth him on a pinnacle of the temple, And saith unto him, if thou be the Son of God, cast thyself down: for it is written He shall give his angels charge concerning thee: and in their hands they shall bear thee up, lest at any time thou dash thy foot against a stone." Wow, well now she knew that these thoughts were just the devil up to his old tricks, and she could resist just as Jesus did.

Reba Jean went back out to the patio, but sitting on the swing did not calm her as it used to, and soon, she found herself pacing and snapping at the dogs. She took a fly swatter to a murder hornet on the side of the house, and it vanished. That scared her into thinking that maybe it wasn't really a hornet, but some evil scout sent to spy on her. How did something that big and nasty disappear after being 'thwacked'?

She barely noticed that she had not even checked on Lady Jane and almost forgot about her. It seemed more as if she just wanted to survive each day and not even continue her quest for treasure.

Reba Jean stomped back inside and sat down. She slanted her eyes at all the notebooks that she used to keep track of everything to help her feel in control. Why on earth did she need four notebooks? Why did it only take four notebooks though to feel like she was in control? She also knew that she still had not had her actual devotions today… again. This was not to be a pattern forming, so why did it feel like a battle just to read her beloved Bible? Ok, fine, she would go through her notebooks, catch up on whatever she felt was not being notated, and then she needed to read her devotions before bedtime. It was late, she was cranky, she needed more rest, and she had been nearly crippled from this week's workload. Her husband was irate when he couldn't fix her pain issues; he had been clueless all this time until she couldn't hide it anymore.

The dogs started barking, again, and the resentment grew along with anger; she was still harboring some rats in the living room it seemed. Defiantly, she caught up on her record keeping of menus, tasks, schedules, and minutiae that she felt like she had to keep track of on paper since her brain was often too fried to remember. Now it was time to have her devotions before the day ended. She still felt frustrated that the past couple of days it seemed so hard to just sit down and have her devotions time. This was usually one of the first things she did every day and looked forward to it. The scant times that she didn't were usually few and far between, but this was the second day in less than a week.

Sure, she prayed and meditated on Scripture and listened to preaching, but to continue her study in Scripture and take notes and glean nuggets was such a delight to her, usually. She picked at a scab on her face and realized her Bible was in the other room. Scowling, she inwardly stomped to the other room very annoyed indeed. How utterly tiresome and inconvenient of her to put it out of reach. Oh, she was very much aware that this was probably all due to utter exhaustion, but her attitude was going to need to be adjusted before she became shipwrecked with the rats again or worse.

Reba Jean finished her devotions and mulled over what she had read. Some of it had pricked her, and she needed to examine those pricks further. Was she guilty of those? The reoccurring statement in the chapter had been "I am the LORD." It grabbed her by the heart as she asked the Lord whether she was maybe not putting Him first or maybe she needed to love Him more intensely than she was.

Her head began to ache as she pondered the commands in Scripture that she had just read. Rubbing her chin and making sure the scab she had picked wasn't bleeding, she sat nearly lost in thought. There was indeed something bugging her, but she just couldn't seem to figure out what it was. Were more sleep and rest the actual answer? She truly hoped it was as easy as that.

The plague was still rampant, and her Monday morning lecture was canceled again. Her husband had declared that she needed to take the day off, even from work. Then he proceeded to list all the things that he hoped to accomplish while he was off. She wanted to laugh, cry, or scream; he never did anything without needing her help. Her day of rest would be at the mercy of whatever whim he decided he needed to do. She kept announcing that she was going to run away; maybe she truly needed a day alone. Was that even right, to want a day away from her home and husband? She could find Scripture to back it up, but was it more that she wasn't relying on God to help her through as He had done just this last week?

She saw a quick note to Lady Jane sent by Lady Constance, and it had the same sentiments that Reba Jean had just been thinking about. Taking a break was ok if it meant that you were focusing more on the Lord during that break. However, she needed to get this note to Lady Jane, and she did not even know where said Lady was! She rubbed a hand over her eyes and thought that searching for Lady Jane would have to wait until the morrow. It was late and she needed to sleep; besides, entering the library at this time of night seemed downright scary!

Could she sleep though, she wondered, if she did not know where Lady Jane was or if she was safe? Sigh, a late-night excursion into the library in hopes that Lady Jane had returned was probably the only way she was going to get any peaceful sleep. Maybe she should send the puppy in and track her scent? The puppy, though, was asleep already, it had gotten tired of waiting for Reba Jean to go to bed. She wondered if, however, any movement from her position would arouse the sleeping pup. The big dog whoofed outside as if to say, "Let me help search."

Reba Jean felt the goosebumps already on her arms as she slid silently through the secret passage up to the library. Creeping in seemed to be the only suitable way to enter this place at such a time of night. The echoes from the big dog barking could still be heard as if it sensed danger and was warning her to be careful. Her eyes got blurry in the dim light, and she rubbed them in hopes to see more clearly. Light gently shimmered from the oil lamp glinting off the gold on the sword by the Ancient One. A steady hum was heard from Sir Theo's library, but a very odd squeaking sound was coming from the surrounding walls of the atrium. She shivered, "Oh, Lord, please don't let there be any rats left in here," she breathed a silent prayer. Straining her ears, she shivered even more as she could not figure out what was causing this new sonic invasion of her library.

She literally felt frozen in fear. Shivering almost violently, she stood stock still, unsure how to proceed. Then with a gulp, she inched forward towards the sound, hoping to discover that it was nothing instead of "something." She found herself against a wall and felt a cold draft and the sound was more like the chirping of a cricket. She calmed down and then felt a lump in her throat. Oh no, what if instead of rats, the underworld had sent crickets to spy on her? She reminded herself to be very careful what she thought about, especially in the library; she had no desire to meet up with some plague of crickets because she couldn't keep it to herself. Ok, crickets; now, where was Lady Jane?

Lady Jane often resorted to the portico the puppy had shown her; much time had been spent dilly-dallying on the swing, daydreaming in the soft breeze, and listening to the faint strains that rippled from the music chamber. She felt very disconnected from the library or any other part of the house. She had not seen Reba Jean in quite a few days, but she honestly did not mind. Reba Jean seemed to always be frustrated or causing drama lately. Here in the conservatory, she felt safe and insulated from anything that Reba Jean was involved in.

Humming to herself, she swung a leg back and forth to keep the swing on its gentle sway. The puppy visited every so often but did not stay very long. She often heard the other creatures in the zoo, but she learned to ignore them. It was like having a mini vacation here in the room of daydreams. Her head began to ache. That was odd; she felt as if she was being pulled out of her daydream and into another place, and she sure hoped it wasn't Reba Jean's reality. The barking of the big dog was louder and more insistent, and she felt goosebumps rise on her arms, that just moments before had been bathed in soft, warm, gentle breezes.

Inhaling deeply, Lady Jane tried to wish herself back into the conservatory of daydreams, back to the gentle sway of the swing or the rocking chair. Either one was always comfortable to her, for she did not wish to be disturbed. Shivering even harder, she reluctantly looked around to see where she was. The lovely portico was gone, and its conservatory was replaced with cold stone walls and the sound of crickets. She couldn't stop shivering and began to make her way to her boudoir where she hoped to find a blanket to wrap herself up in. Her head hurt even more, and she felt like someone else was in the library with her. Looking around in hopes it was Mercy and Goodness, she felt a presence draw closer and she gulped down a scream. Cold hands touched her face and felt her chin, and she shuddered, her hands too shaky to defend herself from this nearly invisible cold intruder.

The cold hands were shivering and shaking just as hard as Lady Jane's were, and it would have been funny if there wasn't such an intense feeling of fear coursing through the room.

A whisper was barely heard, "Who are you?"

Lady Jane thought it sounded like Reba Jean, but she wasn't sure, and neither did she trust anything or anyone. Lady Jane thought she would be funny and replied, "You can call me Cordelia."

A snort answered her, and suddenly Reba Jean began to laugh almost hysterically. She had found Lady Jane, and they had scared each other enough to last a lifetime. Reba Jean gripped her friend's arm tightly and whispered in her ear, "You nearly made me wet myself! I am so glad I found you, but now I have to run to the water closet!"

A few short moments later, Reba Jean returned, embraced Lady Jane, and then declared that she needed to go to bed, but they should really have a talk, and very soon. The puppy appeared, whining about their feet. Reba Jean picked up the pitiful puppy and, resignedly, knew it was time to head to bed. The puppy was shivering just as much as they were. Why was it shivery cold in the library? The sound of the crickets stopped, and both women looked at each other wide-eyed. The lack of sound was just as alarming as when it was non-stop.

The puppy sniffed Reba Jean and tried to get comfortable in her arms as it just wanted to go back to sleep. The sound of water could be heard, and both women turned to the fountain of living water in the middle of the atrium. It was such a comforting sound, and Reba Jean closed her eyes in relief. She snuggled the puppy closer and turned to Lady Jane bidding her a good night. It was a relief to have found her, but figuring out where she had been all this time would have to keep until another day.

Lady Jane watched her mistress and the puppy slip into the secret hatch in the floor and disappear out of her sight. She wandered aimlessly around the fountain trailing her fingers in the lovely, silvery water. She made her rounds to each of the treasured artifacts and peeked into chambers and corridors as she made her way to her boudoir. She hoped that she could sleep, something that she was still getting used to being able to do after all these years. Sleep did not come easy or fast even if Reba Jean took a sleeping potion. She noticed her goosebumps had disappeared, and she had stopped shivering. She was totally going to blame Reba Jean for that nonsense!

Tomorrow she would have to catch up with Reba Jean and surely, they would continue their quest for treasure, wouldn't they? Maybe though, she could sidle back into her new retreat in the conservatory in the portico on the side of the library. With that delicious thought in mind, she closed her eyes upon her settee and willed herself to have sweet dreams. Half asleep, she pulled up a soft comforter over her shoulders and felt her breathing deepen and her body relax and grow limp. Ahh, this was almost as good as daydreaming on the swing.

Reba Jean felt her shivers and goosebumps subside, but the puppy was still shivering, it was way past bedtime. She still felt a bit out of sorts and hoped that maybe a good night's sleep would fix whatever was causing her head to ache and her spirit to feel out of sorts. She wasn't sure if she had anything to confess, and she was still mulling over some of the verses she had read earlier for her devotions. She would need to talk to her Heavenly Father about those.

Taking her sleeping elixir, she snatched up the shaking puppy once again and headed for the bedroom. She would bid her husband a good night and pray that she would sleep long and hard. This actually had happened, for once. Her sleep had been good, but her thoughts were further disturbed the next day by her continued reading in Leviticus. There was no hindrance to her reading the Bible that morning, but she was struck by how very carnal and compromising her sphere of Christianity was in this day and time. She knew there was no way she would have made it as an ancient Jew. Of course, maybe if she had been raised in that system, that might have made a difference. It was repeated throughout her reading to be holy, to be clean, and to be separated. She had been raised very strictly, but it was more for appearance's sake it seemed, than for sanctification. If no one was watching or would find out, then it was okay to be lenient in some areas. Other things that you would think would be the right thing to do, were abhorred. She never understood the thought process or lack thereof in the decisions that went into her upbringing.

Chapter 11

The day progressed in a much better fashion than she had even expected, catching up on housework, resting as much as possible, and trying to be compassionate towards the zoo inmates. Her husband puttered around and took off to run errands as he was prone to do on his day off. They really had such diverse opinions of how a day off should be defined. She had spoken to a sweet friend yesterday, who could tell she was obviously not feeling well. She had serious health issues with similar results, so she was already fussing about Reba Jean getting a real doctor to check out her issues. Reba Jean had a feeling there was something going on, but between age, menopause, and weight, who would look beyond the surface to discover if she was going to live in pain all her life, or just a phase she was passing through?

Reba Jean took the puppy outside yet again and wandered around inspecting things on the patio. She had heard weird sounds last night and again this morning, one of the reasons she was cleaning everything she could today in hopes to figure out where the noises came from and why. She found the murder hornet she had indeed killed last night, laying on the patio floor. That was a relief, but the source of the odd noises had not been discovered. The crickets were even silent today; she was beginning to wonder if she was losing her sanity, for real.

As she sat and stewed over the mystery, she realized that she had not even been up to the library today. Did Lady Jane get any rest? Were those noises emanating from the library and not the lower levels of the house? Just thinking about those sounds sent a shudder through her frame. She did not feel well, was it all the food, the exhaustion, or something else causing that sour pit in the bottom of her stomach? Reba Jean sat as still as she could, except for that left leg jiggling up and down. The only outward sign of the restlessness within, she wanted to savor this moment of solitude and serenity. Why wasn't the serenity felt inside? If it was, then her leg wouldn't be sending warning signals that all was not well.

She could seriously go for a cream soda, but alas, she had drunk the last of those yesterday. The dog yipped from behind the closed kitchen door. She had just wanted a few moments without the puppy clinging to her like a tumor. Indeed, her thoughts and feelings were not very serene; it was just a shallow appearance of calm. She had a feeling that the DIY show on tv was not as peace-filled as listening to music that sang praises to the Lord. She wondered if she was really more like King Saul and less like David, the shepherd. Her leg increased its jiggling, but she couldn't put a finger on what the issues were that needed resolving. Her heart and mind felt fairly calm; was it an illusion?

Her stomach still felt upset, maybe it was food related. Reba Jean went on a search through the kitchen for something to take that feeling away. Her mind flitted briefly to the treasure hunt she had started weeks ago and had left unfinished in the middle of the quest. She knew that once you found treasure you had to guard it and let it change your life in a more profitable way. Where was the excitement and zeal to finish the quest? Wow, she sure was full of questions! That reminded her again of the lecture she had given to the fledgling librarians a few months ago. When life is full of questions, look at the question mark, and ask, "What Quest Am I On?" The "?" itself showed that life often is a curve or a detour before you get to your stopping place at the end. Life is never a straight line. Was it the curves that she was having to maneuver through that were causing her hesitation? What quest was she on?

Reba Jean spent the next few days hunting down the cause of the cricket noises, and then the horrid clunking sound that had started. It always sounded as if something had fallen into the sink, a cacophony of metal and glass. It wasn't too long before she conquered most of her fear and stood still long enough to ferret out the cause. It was the used refrigerator they had purchased; it sounded like crickets when it was running, then as it shut off it emitted a screeching, grinding kerchunk. She mentioned it to her husband who also had silently wondered at the noise that often awoke him out of sound sleep. Even though she now knew the cause, it still was quite alarming when you hear such a "clunk" in the middle of a quiet house. She wasn't losing her mind, just her patience.

Her second job was going to start next week; she was still praying her way out of it. However, she had also started praying her way through it so that God would get honor and glory somehow. Her desire for the treasure hunt was renewed after listening to her pastor's Wednesday night message. Her study of Leviticus however was very sobering. She knew she deserved death under the law—only God's grace and mercy kept her alive. At the thought of mercy, she had a sudden desire to run up to the library. Not heeding her recent undercover missions, she bounded up the staircase as she used to do. Wrenching open the door that had not been used in a very long time, it emitted a squawk that drowned out any chime that might have sounded.

The noise was reminiscent of the refrigerator, and Lady Jane was startled out of a daydream. She grabbed the golden sword and came running to see who was breaking in! Sword raised, she raced through the atrium and brandished the sword in the air as she arrived at the entrance. Reba Jean threw her arms up in a futile attempt to shield herself from the library's avenging guardian. The golden sword, however, as it is a discerner of the thoughts and intents of the heart, did no harm as it passed through Reba Jean with its double-edged blade. Reba Jean gaped wide-eyed at Lady Jane who collapsed in sobs when she saw her mistress. Goodness and Mercy came alongside and ministered to both women.

They struggled to recover from their fright, sputtering out apologies, regrets, and consolations. Reba Jean's heart was racing. She had wanted to see Mercy, and she got her desire fulfilled in quite an unexpected manner! Gulping a few more times, she tried to regain her composure. She had not been harmed by the golden sword, but she definitely felt it go through her flesh and marrow. Lady Jane took longer to recover. She had tried to murder her mistress!

Reba Jean looked up to the golden dust motes and pulled a few towards her, with a few fumbling motions she fashioned a lovely shawl out of the pliable golden strands she had stretched. Wrapping Lady Jane in the warm, golden shawl, she took her hand and tucking it in her own, she pulled her along as she walked to the fountain of living water in the middle of the atrium. With a couple of droplets that she dribbled on Lady Jane's brow, she was able to further calm the sobbing woman.

Lady Jane sat on the edge of the fountain and watched her beloved mistress continue to run her fingers through the water. The beautiful sunshine from the bejeweled windows overhead cast prisms of light around the room as they shone through the crystalline water. Reba Jean watched the prisms dance, and then with a thought of something that had happened earlier in the week she gathered up a droplet. Fastening a thin strand of gold from one of the dust motes to it, she hung it suspended in the air catching the light and casting prisms of promise all over the room.

Grasping Lady Jane by the hand, she practically dragged her down the corridor of hope toward the nursery. They did not go in, but Reba Jean whispered to herself excitedly. Lady Jane thought she could discern the words, hope, promise, and treasure. Reba Jean spun Lady Jane around in circles until they were both dizzy and laughing. Lady Jane got the hiccups and found herself sprawled against the wall of the corridor gasping for air. Reba

Jean looked around dreamily and wondered about a Scripture verse that the Preacher had read from the other night.

Before Lady Jane could even catch her breath, Reba Jean had sprinted off to the Ancient One, leaving Lady Jane in the corridor of hope looking at the entrance to the nursery. As Reba Jean neared the beloved copy of Scripture up here in the library, she heard it already flipping its pages, anticipating her search. She read Hebrews 6 and there, highlighted in lovely golden hues were verses 18-19, "That by two immutable things, in which it was impossible for God to lie, we might have a strong consolation, who have fled for refuge to lay hold upon the hope set before us: Which hope we have as an anchor of the soul, both sure and steadfast, and which entereth into that within the veil."

Reba Jean needed that steadfastness, and the words consolation and refuge struck a deep chord in her, as well. However, it was the anchor of hope that caught her mind visually. She was on a treasure hunt, a quest to find incorruptible things of value to seek out and obtain. Her salvation was only the first such treasure; she had nearly forgotten the treasure list she had made so many weeks ago. She had her blessing book, yet again it lay untouched. She had the corridor of hope, but that was specifically about the grandbaby; she needed something more tangible and steadfast. The thought of that horrible day at sea with Captain Insidious came to mind. She needed an anchor that she could hold on to.

Looking around, she almost wished she had a few misty tendrils dangling like they used to do. She felt a light tap on her arm; a golden dust mote had requested her attention. She laughed; how silly of her. She had made so many things with the golden dust motes; they were the perfect material for this symbolic anchor of hope. With her consent, the golden dust motes began forming a very large, strong, golden anchor. The intricate filigree was beautiful, but the strength of it was undeniable. Before they were finished, she wondered where it should be placed in the

95

library. Casting about, she realized that Lady Jane had not joined her from the corridor of hope.

A bit puzzled by her absence, she left the golden anchor being crafted and went to search for Lady Jane. The Lady was no longer in the corridor, and upon further search, was seemingly nowhere to be found, again!

"Lady Jane?!" Reba Jean called out half frantic, half mystified. Where had she gotten off to now? Reba Jean waited for a reply even as she began racing through aisles of books and through dusty corridors. Straining her ears, all she could hear was the lovely hymns playing in the music chamber. Why wouldn't the guardian of the library stay where she was supposed to? "Oh, Lady Jane, wherefore art thou?!" sang out Reba Jean.

The Lady Jane had returned to her portico of peace, and the puppy had joined her happily as it had entered through the main entrance of the library, whose door was still thrown wide open. The two had entered the calm conservatory, and each had flopped in their favorite spots. Lady Jane had collapsed onto the swing watching the hummingbirds and butterflies. The puppy had begun rolling around in sheer happiness to be in their new favorite room.

Reba Jean spotted the main door of the library wide open, and she completely panicked. Had Lady Jane been captured, or....? Surely, Lady Jane wouldn't, couldn't leave the library, could she? Was she even now in the living room? She had ended up on a pirate ship, maybe she could just totally leave and never return! Hyperventilating, Reba Jean couldn't even call out to Lady Jane. She debated on slamming shut the door but resorted to putting the golden sword in the entrance. That ought to keep out any nefarious villains, without harming the rightful occupants.

Security measures in place, Reba Jean began a systematic search of the library, aisle by aisle, rooms, corridors, hunting for Lady Jane. Finally, she noticed a corridor on the outskirts of the library along the new stone facing, which was dusty except for a couple of sets of footprints. Upon further inspection, she realized that one of the sets was puppy paw prints. Mystified, she followed the prints and discovered the lovely portico, the conservatory that Lady Jane and the puppy escaped to ever since they found it.

Reba Jean exhaled all her pent-up emotions and let herself completely relax with the idyllic breeze floating around them. She flopped down in a rocker, and the puppy came over to greet her. Lady Jane almost felt frustrated that her place of peace had been discovered by the mistress of mayhem, as she often considered Reba Jean's title to be. The peace, however, was so soothing that Reba Jean closed her eyes and began daydreaming. What an ideal spot to write her book, she thought to herself. Now, she understood why Lady Jane couldn't or maybe wouldn't respond to her calls.

The breeze put them all to sleep, like a lazy summer afternoon was wont to do. Reba Jean found herself dreaming of a room filled with treasure, and Lady Jane dreamed she was a princess in Egypt with servants fanning her with large ostrich plumes. The puppy, well who knows what it dreamed, at least it wasn't a nightmare. They spent the afternoon in the portico of peace, or was it the conservatory of contentment, Reba Jean really wasn't sure what its official title should be labeled.

It was as if the entire library, or even the world, had hit the pause button here in this room of daydreams. Reba Jean felt her foot fall asleep under her, and that tingly sensation brought her back to her senses. She had left the anchor, the treasure hunt, and even her book all unfinished as she lollygagged here in this bucolic scene. However, this peace was a gift from God and part of her treasure. She would need to make sure this room was secure and steadfast, and only accessible by the rightful recipients of the gift.

Reba Jean laconically rose to her feet and leaving Lady Jane and the puppy in the peaceful portico, she retraced her steps back to the golden dust motes. A huge, heavy golden anchor welcomed her entrance back to the main section of the library. Reba Jean was not sure where it should be placed, so she left it suspended from floor to ceiling right where it had been so artfully crafted. Pulling a book off one of the library shelves, she opened the ancient-looking tome and began writing therein.

The words appeared as a list of treasures from God that she had acquired thus far:

Salvation
Peace
Prayer
Praise
Promises
Scripture
Souls saved
Hope
Blessings

She wondered if she had forgotten anything in her list, or what she was still missing. Inspection of the list left her awestruck. These were so valuable to her, she hoped she never lost track of them, or lost sight of their worth.

Knowing how remiss she had been, she closed the ancient tome and opened up her blessing book; she needed to record the salvation of one she had earnestly prayed over and for. She also wanted to thank God for His reminders that He was listening to her by sending her messages that kept her on this quest, this journey. He also sent reminders of His promises and His faithfulness to those promises. A nasty fly landed nearby, and she realized that the library door was still wide open. Now that she knew where Lady Jane was, it was time to secure the library from intruders.

The library door slammed shut, the golden sword was returned to its place near the lovely marble table holding the Ancient One. She caressed the gossamer table runner under the glowing oil lamp in front of the Crimson Vault. Returning to her place by the Ancient One, with the tinkling sound of crystalline water flowing from the fountain of living water, she began to pen her words of thanksgiving in her blessing book. With pen poised, she was interrupted by the whining of the puppy.

Her expression soured, as the puppy began jumping on her, clearly wanting to be held. The puppy sneezed repeatedly in her lap, and she found the act of trying to write very difficult. She was beginning to wonder if this puppy had been a tool used by the underworld to disrupt her sanity and peace. With a determined set to her face, she found a couch and sat down with the puppy and her blessing book. The puppy began chewing on something, while she began to write down the things that she was thankful to God for. Then, the puppy began chewing on her blessing book! She calmed it down and stroked its head, distracting it from chewing up her treasure. There was an application in there for sure. The blessing book could be destroyed, but the blessings would still be there, nothing could take away something that God had already given her. The thought of that welled up inside of her; that meant joy and peace were not lost or stolen either! The music from the chamber began to swell and surround her as she continued to thank God for His blessings on her. The sweet odor of praise filled the entire library, as the strains of "Nearer My God to Thee" began to crescendo and echo throughout.

Reba Jean closed her blessing book, still ruminating over the recent blessings that she had recorded just now. The puppy hung off the arm of the couch half asleep, again. She knew she probably should work on her book or do housework, but the sweet smell was like a loving hug wrapping its arms around her and she did not want to lose contact with all that was holy to take care of the mundane.

Lady Jane followed her nose back to the atrium of the library; such a heavenly smell permeated her senses. The puppy whined at her entrance and then laid back down on the arm of the sofa. Hymns of praise swelled and flowed around them, golden dust motes danced, and prismed rainbows danced heavenly hues around the room and bounced off the stone walls. Oh, why couldn't it be like this all the time? Yet she knew she needed to treasure every moment of this while it lasted.

The puppy grew insistent, and Reba Jean knew she needed to return to the rest of her duties. She bid a fond farewell to Lady Jane, and she and the puppy exited the library through the main door, remembering to shut it securely behind them. The treasures in the library needed to be kept safe, even if they were just symbols of the real treasure. The visual reminders were of value in this earthly realm to remember what God gives to His children who are faithful servants.

Reba Jean played with the large dog for a short time, and then let her mind wander as it was often prone to do. She found herself picking away at the scab on her face yet again and remembered when she was the cause of the scar on Lady Jane's sweet face. That memory struck her as she realized that her persistent sore was in the same spot as Lady Jane's scar. Her heart thudded with the realization that they were probably connected. She did not like her own appearance and even when she looked half way decent in her estimation she still felt frumpy and unattractive. The sore on her face did not help matters, but she needed to stop thinking about herself.

Coming into the house, she locked the puppy down in the den in hopes that she could work on her second book for a while before supper. The puppy yipped, her face itched, the air was cold, and her ear ached. Of course, any time she wanted to be productive something superficial would exert itself trying to distract her. She was so short on patience these days already. She nearly whined to God how she longed for the days where it was serene and peace-filled like it was earlier in the portico off the library.

She needed to bottle up that peace and stick her nose in it every time she felt like she was going to scream. *Hmm, was that possible?* she mused to herself. She felt a shadow slink behind her chair and felt the hairs on her neck stand at attention. Looking around, she saw it was only a cat craving attention. She was getting tired of having a zoo, and soon she would be adding additional responsibilities, a second job. The puppy yipped, that cat tried to cuddle on top of the laptop and her Bible, and she gave up trying to get anything done.

After some more play time outside, she re-entered the house to hear the precious sounds of the orchestrated hymn yet again playing "Blessed Assurance." It seemed to be on a short loop today, as she had heard it played a few times already since turning it on. "Echoes of mercy, whispers of love..." those words caught her attention. Oh, now she understood why it was playing so often. The Lord was reminding her during her short-tempered moments that He still had mercy and love to help her through all this.

Chapter 12

Captain Insidious had been biding his time. He couldn't seem to breach the defenses of the library, so he just stirred up the animals and situations around Reba Jean. Her lack of patience was so gratifying to him. Today, however, the library door was thrust wide open, but before he could assemble his troop, he sent a lone fly in to observe. It made it through the door in the nick of time before that hated golden sword of the King was placed on guard at the main entrance.

He used the proverbial fly-on-the-wall method, however, to scope out the changes to the library in hopes he could figure out what all this treasure gibberish was all about. The fly escaped death by hiding on the gray stone walls, and soon, it had enough information to report back to Captain Insidious.

It flew out of the library unnoticed as Reba Jean exited with the puppy. Its report deepened Captain Insidious' standard scowl. Pondering all the security measures, the artifacts, and the new symbols in place in the library, he stroked his cheek with his talon-like fingers. With a gleam in his reptilian eyes, he plucked a book out of midair, and with his talon, he scooped a glob of black tarry ooze to use as ink. Reba Jean might have her half-used blessing book, but he was going to replace it with the Book of Regrets!

He began to write his list of her supposed regrets in a column just like the fly had reported her blessings had been recorded. He felt intense satisfaction that this book was obviously going to be more used than that dusty old tome of blessings that she always set aside. He placed the zoo, the jobs, her looks, and her health on the top of the list. He needed to keep her thinking about herself, then he could easily steal her sanity, steadfastness, security, and all the other deliciously wicked "s" words he had applied to her case.

Reba Jean found herself outside yet again. She struggled to be thankful for the life she had, but she was feeling tortured by the constant need for attention from everyone and everything. She went back into the house and locked the puppy in the den. Its yips grated on her nerves, as she waited for her supper to finish baking in the oven. Her home used to be a refuge, an oasis, now she just wanted to run away, or at least send all the animals and people away.

The dishes were done, and she had no desire to work on laundry. Reba Jean grumbled nearly as loudly as her stomach. So, she analyzed, peace wasn't necessarily being stolen, but it sure was getting smothered. The storm clouds outside the window reflected her own internal turmoil. The SON was shining, but the storm clouds were right there swelling up in front of the Son. She felt her features turn down into a grimace, and she sulked for a few minutes. Pushing herself to her feet, she went to check on the food; maybe she was just hungry. Sleep and food seemed to really mess with her when not applied in the right amounts at the right time. The puppy was so upset at being locked in with its food, toys, and water. She wished she could have that predicament.

Her supper was ready, she waited for it to cool and wondered how Adam and Noah dealt with all the animals they were in charge of for so long. The puppy yipped with a high-pitched whine, and she felt her heart cringe and her blood pressure rise. She refused to give in; the puppy was going to be in the den next week a lot more often with her second job; it needed to get used to not being attached to her like an umbilical cord. Trying to tune out the puppy and concentrate on the hymns playing, she worked some more on her second book.

A bite of her food burned the roof of her mouth as it was still too hot to be eaten; that was going to leave a mark, as usual.

104

Her peaceful day just seemed to evaporate into endless frustrations. She eyed the storm clouds hovering outside; they hadn't really changed, just hovered. If she could only get two more pages written in her book this next chapter would be finished. *Would anyone read her books?* she wondered. She needed to ask Lady Jane how she was going to communicate with the Lady Constance if she was "out of pocket" for the next few months.

She already messaged Mardie, received no reply, and surmised that no one was interested in reading the book that they were even written into the plot. The dogs began barking, and Reba Jean felt like the storm clouds had moved into her own mind.

As she pouted, refusing to acknowledge the dogs who craved attention. She wondered why she had to say "yes" to everyone who needed something from her. She felt so used and felt also that if she said "no" then she wasn't being very Christ-like. Why was saying no to things considered so selfish in her Christian circles? As the Apostle Paul said, not everything was expedient for him to do. Yet, here she was often saying yes to things without praying for God's will concerning whether she should be the answer to everyone's problems. Her supper had cooled sufficiently, in fact, was cooling too fast, such an illustration of her walk with the Lord. She was on fire one minute, and lukewarm to cold the very next, literally. The strains of "I Need Thee Every Hour" broke through her frustrated mental misery. She stopped and listened to the Lord speaking to her, and even the puppy hushed for a moment or two. Reba Jean closed her eyes and mentally sang the lyrics to the hymn along with the orchestrated sounds filtering through the kitchen.

Her stomach was in knots; she didn't think it was the food. More likely, it was the stress induced by her thoughts and the whining and barking of the dogs. She compared their barks to the ringing of the phone; it was programmed into a person that it required immediate attention or something alarming might happen if ignored. She thought she needed to re-train the zoo, but maybe she needed to re-train herself. Her husband felt like his life wasn't complete without animals around, except he was hardly around the animals. She sorely disagreed with him on that philosophy. Her mother might not have wanted animals because of their mess, and she did not like to clean the house but once a week. Reba Jean didn't want animals because they craved her attention and made unnecessary noise.

Tamping down her storm of frustration and regret, she put her plate and glass in the sink and figured she would jump on social media to see what she could see. The other song that kept looping through the orchestration today was "Be Thou My Vision." She had a feeling that God was trying to tell her something through that song, as well. She needed to stop looking at her situation and start looking at the only ONE Who could help her survive her own storm.

The storm was apt to brew at the slightest provocation. The triggers were usually the dogs, or sometimes as an empath she absorbed others' frustrations, and they triggered her own. She was having sleeping issues even with the sleep aids, and she knew this had a bearing on her ability to handle stress.

It was like a vicious cycle that never seemed to end. If the living room was always in turmoil and chaos, it was bound to affect the library. She used to believe that the library affected the living room, that it started up there, but now, she really began to consider that the library only reflected whatever was happening down here in the living room. The living room was the heart of the home; if the heart was not working correctly, it would affect all areas of the home. It was more than just a house, it was a home, and furthermore, the temple of God, Who chose to dwell therein.

Reba Jean stewed over these thoughts. Yes stewed, not pondered or meditated, quite literally stewed. She could pontificate all she wanted, even help others with their problems, quote Scripture and pray, but there seemed to be no end to her own personal battles. Oh, God was not silent, but she seemed to be stewing in her own juices, not really having the victory over anything. She had moments of peaceful help, but they lasted only as long as there was a calm. Her Pastor's wife had likened faith to a roller coaster ride, if our faith was only as strong as our circumstances then we were going to be in for a nail-biting ride.

Aching to write more, and to hash out the storyline in her second book, it seemed like she was thwarted at every turn. There was so much that she wanted to express in this second book, yet it just seemed all jumbled up, wanting to burst out like some chemistry experiment gone horribly wrong. She had prayed for clarity. She had it all visualized in her head, but when she shut out the pestering noisy animals and started the music playing, her mind seemed to seize up on her and go blank. Reba Jean's left leg started shaking again; she was mad, restless, frustrated, and yes, stressed.

Chapter 13

Lady Jane gasped and began to run through the library; some bees from Sir Theo's library had gotten loose, except they were acting like murder hornets. They were chasing her, intent on stinging her. She ran screaming and crying. Why would Sir Theo have such murderous bees in his library? Did he command them to chase her and inflict serious harm? Gasping for air, she ducked into the secret conservatory, but there was a swarm there waiting on her! How to escape the angry swarm of murderous bees?

Gulping in some air, Lady Jane looked around frantically, bees, bees, and more bees seemed to be gathering, and she felt like she was the only target they had their sights set upon. King Abba said there would always be a way to escape, but where was the escape hatch? She shrieked and dove under the swing, pulling a blanket down on top of her as a shield. She could feel the bees trying to get their stingers through the fabric. Little pinpricks made her itch and tremble, the little nips of venom made her nauseous. "HELPPPPPP!"

Reba Jean could feel the music competing with the dog barking and the puppy yipping and scratching at the door. She ran her fingers through her hair and just wanted to yank it out. If she kept this up, her blood pressure would sky rocket again. Her preacher was going through some of the same issues, and he had decided to just keep going as much as he could. She had determined that if her preacher could keep functioning, then so could she, right? She felt a grumble start somewhere deep in her chest; she was so beyond finished with dogs, jobs, and people.

They were always expecting her to do everything for them. Yes, it was very un-Christlike of her, she was sure, at least that is what had been ingrained into her. Scripture even said she was to be "given to hospitality."

The glimmer of a thought about Philippians 4:8 and what she should be thinking about came into her mind, but she squashed it. There was nothing lovely or just or good report going on for her to think about right now. She realized she had tucked her jiggly leg under her so that it was not shaking up and down anymore. Yet inwardly she was still very restless, her head was starting to hurt and that was not a good sign. The puppy kept yipping, and Reba Jean felt a scream welling up in her throat. Her skin was getting itchy, she felt like she was allergic to something, probably her life.

The book was not going along in its storyline how she had envisioned it in her head just the last couple of days. The words of victory that she wanted to share with her readers seemed to be locked away in a box, and all she could do was spew discontentment onto the pages in front of her. Reba Jean looked to her left and saw the notes from the message about the anchor of hope. The words "it's a living hope, a lasting hope, a lightening hope, and a looking hope" jumped off the page at her where she had scribbled it down that night that felt like months ago instead of less than a week ago. The notes went on to say that this hope should be our message, our motivation, and our ministry. "Ha!" she blurted out loud, "if someone saw me right now, they would say I was acting and thinking pretty hopeless."

She folded her hands and inhaled a breath; she needed to find that anchor of hope, something that was steadfast and sure to hold onto through all this nonsense. Yes, it just felt like sheer nonsense!

Just as her headache seemed to intensify, the puppy yipped in a soprano shriek. She just wanted to run away from home; it was no longer her oasis. It was her fault for saying yes to the puppy, to the extra cats, to the big dog, and to the two jobs. She was in such a juxtaposition. The jobs afforded her the ability to be at home and the pay had definitely been a blessing. However, the jobs took a huge toll on her physically, which then affected her mentally and emotionally.

Just a few short weeks ago, the Lord had been telling her to be still, to wait on Him. She had tried to do that, but there still didn't seem to be anything happening to help her get out of the mess she felt like she had talked herself into. Clasping her hands together again, she tried to calm her breathing, her head was hurting, and she couldn't take more medicine. She had already drunk plenty of water, then the strains of her favorite hymn playing slid into her consciousness. "It Is Well with My Soul." It was well with her soul, just not anything else, it seemed. She focused on the music and sang the lyrics in her head. For a couple of minutes, all was very quiet, she felt herself calming down, and tears threatened to run down her face.

This was so much what she had longed for, worship music, quiet moments, time to reflect and meditate on God. Instead, she seemed to be fighting for her very sanity. Mardie would have told her to take a chill pill. She didn't want more medicine or its side effects; she had enough issues already. She truly believed that there was a way out of this, or through it. She had to hold onto the hope that God would see her through, somehow. Clinging to the brief moment where hope seemed to hold her, she walked down the hallway. She wanted to get away from the sound of the zoo clamoring for her attention.

Reba Jean spent a few moments in her rarely used prayer closet. Oh, she prayed, but never behind the closed door as she would have in the past. She remembered her eyes drifting during the message on Sunday, and they landed on her passage of Scripture that she had been using for her new mindset. Matthew 6:19-21 felt like a sharp reminder of what she was supposed to be thinking about. Then her eyes drifted to the previous page and landed on verses six through eight, especially verse six, "But thou, when thou prayest, enter into thy closet, and when thou hast shut thy door, pray to thy Father which is in secret; and thy Father which seeth in secret shall reward thee openly." It was no mistake that praying in a prayer closet would help her lay up the right kind of treasure in heaven. They were distinctly tied together. She had come home, dug out her prayer journal, and vowed to use it every day along with her blessing book. However, she had not been inside the room that she used as a prayer closet or shut the door to the world.

She only sat for a few minutes. There were too many distractions, but her heart ached for some way to resume this time alone in secret with God. The day went on, her emotions were completely off the charts; she wanted to scream and have a temper tantrum. She was so done with the zoo and their constant need for attention. A storm rumbled in during the afternoon, and it fit her mood. She heard the calm, reassuring hymns reminding her that God was there; she just needed to focus on Him. Sitting down with the whiny puppy, she worked on a jigsaw puzzle; that alone always seemed to calm her down as she listened to the hymns.

A headache started forming, she did not dare check her blood pressure, and she felt like screaming again. Instead, she dug out the notes from the guest preacher's message from the Sunday before. Colossians 2:3 grabbed her attention, "In whom are hid all the treasures of wisdom and knowledge." She was trying to find treasures to hide in her library, but this verse said that only in Him, Jesus Christ, could be found the treasures of wisdom and knowledge. If she wanted those treasures in her library, she needed to get them from Him. That of course was true of all the other treasures; they were not something she could just conjure up herself. Oh, she could swirl golden dust motes together to make symbolic artifacts in the library, but they were only imaginary representations of the real thing. She desperately needed the real treasures in her library, but more so in her living room! The last of her sermon notes directed her to Acts 17:29, "Forasmuch then as we are the offspring of God, we ought not to think that the Godhead is like unto gold, or silver, or stone, graven by art and man's device."

Pondering how that might affect the library and her treasure hunt, she saw more notes that she had randomly kept in her Bible. She was not sure what they were for, so she looked up the verses on them out of curiosity. 1 Chronicles 28:9 "...know thou the God of thy father, and serve him with a perfect heart and with a willing mind: for the LORD searcheth all hearts, and understandeth all the imaginations of the thoughts: if thou seek him, he will be found of thee; but if thou forsake him, he will cast thee off for ever." She knew this was no mistake; these verses were the key to her sanity. She needed to make sure that her symbolic artifacts did not become idols to her or Lady Jane. It was the principle and precepts that the symbols were to visually represent that she needed to seek after, but not to worship, rather to use to draw her focus back to worshipping God. She understood this; she just hoped that somehow it would not be misconstrued or misrepresented.

There was a longer passage that she had noted in Isaiah, so she searched that out to see if she could glean any nuggets from that. The Bible reading was like a salve to her enslaved emotions, so she was hungry for more to keep her from losing her mind. It was chapter fifty-four of Isaiah verses one through thirteen that she read. She knew this had multiple meanings to her, such a picturesque description of God's love and promises. He always kept His promises; oh, what comfort that brought her. Verse eleven felt specific to her, even though it was directed to Israel, "O thou afflicted, tossed with tempest, and not comforted, behold, I will lay thy stones with fair colours, and lay thy foundations with sapphires." Reba Jean was part of His bride, and also His child, so she would get to see this promise fulfilled and

113

kept. That tempest was only temporary, her tossing to and fro would eventually have an end.

Reba Jean's husband came home shortly after her Bible study time, and she went back outside to watch him as he mowed. It was always her duty to move the vehicles back and forth at the right time so that he didn't have to stop the mower. They had it down to an unspoken pattern now. However, today, every time she sat down outside, she felt like she had sat on an ant nest. She itched like crazy, but only outside. The yellow jackets wouldn't leave her alone, and she got so frustrated being outside; she couldn't even enjoy being on the swing!

After supper, she tried to sit down in the stillness of the house to write some more in her second book. Out of the blue, the puppy demanded to be held. It had been fine for the last thirty minutes, but no, every time she wanted to do something, the puppy wanted to be held. She ignored it and hoped it would go pester its master instead. Her husband came out and mentioned the whining, and Reba Jean started listing her complaints about the puppy's behavior. Then she hushed, it sure wouldn't change a bloomin' thing. She had begged God to remove the puppy and the big dog; she had even prayed away her two jobs, but so far, no answer, except just to keep going.

Her husband was thinking of changing jobs and had been for a while. Now he inserted in his discussions about getting one that made enough money that she wouldn't have to work. She wanted to hope that would happen; oh, wouldn't that be glorious? Shame would then come over her; the first job should bring her happiness serving the Lord in this way. However, she ended up seeing the worst habits of church people. She was also concerned that any new job making that much money would keep him away for hours on end or keep him out of church.

She would rather work than have him out of church again. Those had been very dark days when he was away from the House of God. The puppy jumped on her again, and her left leg

114

started jiggling agitatedly. Reba Jean wanted to escape; maybe she could get to the library without the puppy following her. Yeah, right, that never happened these days; that puppy stuck to her like Velcro. She complained to her husband again and managed to get the puppy distracted for like thirty seconds.

Things needed to change before she blew a gasket, so to speak. Now, she was scratching her itches inside. Maybe it was stress and not something physical? The puppy whined and yipped, begging to be held. Thoughts of running up to the library were just not going to come to fruition. She wondered if she could manage to sit on the couch with the puppy and use the laptop, as well. Was it worth a try?

Lady Jane hid under the blanket, but the hornets did not relent in their vicious attack upon her. Screaming, she ran and jumped into the fountain of living water submerging all but the very tip of her nose under. She saw the swarm increase in size and the hornets seemed to grow into oversized monsters straining to get to her as she struggled to remain immersed. Where did these horrible things come from? The only bees she knew of were the ones in Sir Theo's library; surely those would not have metamorphosized into these killing machines?

Reba Jean got ready for church, and suddenly, was verbally assaulted by a barrage of angry questions from her husband. It was all concerning petty issues, but he was fairly livid; if he had not been saved, would he have physically assaulted her? After church, she tried the "soft answer turneth away wrath" method but also told him that he could speak to her in a sweeter tone of voice. His reply dripped like acidic vinegar as he informed her that he was not able to speak to her in anything else but harshness. Reba Jean was heartbroken; what had happened to her husband?

His anger was like a swarm of angry hornets attacking her at every turn. She had a strong idea that somehow Captain Insidious had found a way into her husband's library. This was a very accurate conclusion on Reba Jean's part. Captain Insidious had indeed discovered that he could assault the library and living room by sending an attack from Sir Theo's library. He had sent in a few murder hornets, stirred up Sir Theo's bees, and sent the whole marauding swarm after Lady Jane and Reba Jean. The onslaught continued for the next few days. The damage would be lasting, the bees divided into various soirees, some attacked the chainmail network and began pulling apart the protective layer that the misty tendrils had constructed. Another swarm kept stinging any little bit of Lady Jane they could get to. They had to be careful because the living water would hinder their effectiveness. Lady Jane tried to stay submerged the best she could. Another swarm kept attacking Sir Theo and his library, keeping him from calming down. Captain Insidious loved all the reports he was getting from his hornet squads.

Standing off to one side watching the battle enfold was General Nefarious; he had sent this strategy down through the ranks to Captain Insidious. General Nefarious was not surprised to see his strategy work; he had used it with great success many times. He just had not been aware of Captain Insidious and his onslaught on the library until the reports started trickling in that piqued his own interest. General Nefarious was excited to see if any of his other ideas would also be used. Recognition would be sure to follow if he was able to wreak massive havoc on any of the Celestial King's infantry.

A few agonizing days passed, and Reba Jean was able to finally communicate and assuage her husband's vinegary angst against her. Now he just complained about everything that made him unhappy, but he did not attack her personally. Her second job was too much for her; she found herself whining, complaining, and breaking into tears talking about it. She

116

couldn't do it! Her husband was finally getting fed up with the large dog as well, but he said he would handle it. Today she was supposed to work her second job, but had managed to get an unexpected day off. She practically sobbed her thanks to the Lord. The morning had been such a relief to listen to the lovely hymns, and the zoo was quiet. Very quiet. She read through her book and was in dismay when she realized that she had not been to the library or even checked on the treasures she had supposedly been collecting.

She still itched from the stinging barrage that her husband had unleashed on her, the emotional scars would take longer to heal. Reba Jean felt her sensitive skin itch as she made her way up to the library. Opening the door, she was greeted with an eerie stillness. She could still hear the hymns playing, but they felt like they were fighting something heavy and smothering. Looking around, she saw half-dead bees littering the floor, like a hive had attacked and had descended en masse into the library. Bewildered, Reba Jean continued her survey and brushed off something that seemed to crawl on her face. The light seemed very dim, but then she realized that the misty tendrils were loosed from their chainmail network and were dangling all over again. She gulped and the pit of her stomach heaved with fear.

The library looked like a war zone, which it was yet again, still, always, a never-ending place of upheaval. She heard a faint hiccup, and spinning around, Reba Jean saw tiny odd bubbles in the fountain of living water. Upon further inspection, she realized that Lady Jane was IN the fountain! Reba Jean shivered, and she felt herself crying inwardly. With a shaking hand, she gently reached in and pulled out the very water-logged Lady Jane. The tip of her nose was swollen, and remnants of the hornet attack could still be seen in the swelling bumps all over her figure.

The two women faced each other, completely at a loss for words. They had not anticipated that they could be attacked from Sir Theo's library. Reba Jean wondered if she should build a wall of protection again, but that did not seem like the correct solution. They just didn't know what to do, the attack had dissipated, the murder hornets had left, but Sir Theo's bees were still affected by that nefarious attack. Reba Jean rubbed her face with her hands and felt dejected defeat. Who did she think she was, all this talk about treasure. She couldn't even function on a daily basis and only seemed to drive people to anger with her.

She just couldn't do it anymore; even trusting God seemed too hard. Her blood pressure may never recover. This last attack from her husband had sent it almost to stroke level, and he didn't seem to take it seriously. Reba Jean curled within herself and completely seemed to ignore Lady Jane. Lady Jane looked around at the seemingly insurmountable mess, Reba Jean, the artifacts, and the dangling misty tendrils that were no longer controlled or secure. Lady Jane looked to see what the priority should be; divide and conquer just like the hornet swarm had done. She remembered a short while back that Lady Constance had come to visit, and Reba Jean had joined them as they discussed their similar issues. They both desired that their marriages needed to be awe-filled, not awful. Reba Jean had commented that the letter "E" seemed to be the missing key to making that happen. So, what words that started with the letter "E" could be used to put their marriages back together?

Lady Constance made a list: Encourage, Excellent, Enjoy, Excited, and Energy. Reba Jean had not made her own list. Maybe that is what Reba Jean needed to do, make a list of things that she could do for her marriage. She just wanted to scream! Then she realized that the letter "E" was in the middle of "scream." Lady Jane pulled a misty tendril towards her along with a book and began to write suggestions for Reba Jean to look over later. Reba Jean, however, still seemed to be in her self-preservation mode.

Reba Jean felt numb, yet tingly, all over; she was only vaguely aware of Lady Jane writing. The misty tendrils were just dangling around like frayed bits of yarn, and the atmosphere just seemed musty and stale. She felt almost paralyzed, the damage just seemed too much, and her desire for treasure, sheer nonsense. A tremor shook her body, but the light in her eyes was just a flicker. Angry hornets, overwhelming stress, high blood pressure, and recurring abominable suggestions had taken their toll on her. She saw the bites all over her body, she had visible signs of the attack, but inwardly they were much more damaging.

Reba Jean sat on the hard floor of the library nearly oblivious to everything; she didn't even try to pray or remember Scripture. She felt like Elijah of old and just wanted to hide and sleep. She could not deal with any of this any longer. A lone tear slid down her cheek unheeded and unchecked. Like a zombie, she lurched to her feet and left the library, she had no strength to do anything about the aftermath.

Chapter 14

Reba Jean barely made it through the next few days. She no longer checked her blood pressure; it would never be normal again. Her husband seemed to be slightly improved, and he even said he would take care of the issues with the big dog. The words "Be Still" had come back around, and she wondered if God was truly going to intervene and help her through this. She had no desire to hunt treasure or even fix the library. She felt as if the living room and library needed to be closed and put out of business. Oh yes, there were a lot of things that she thought about, and sometimes even said aloud that "supposed" Christians weren't supposed to think or say.

She endured a day with her parents and often wondered why she wasn't dead yet from the disrespect and lack of honor that she felt toward them. She really wondered why God had allowed her to be born into their care if all it did was breed resentment and disgust. She realized that her mother had the same goals in life as her grandmother on her paternal side. Yet, the two of them never liked each other no matter how much they were alike.

Reba Jean went through the motions of the weekly lecture, but it felt just a bit off. She went to visit Mardie and left dissatisfied with that excursion. There seemed to be a lot of discontentment, and even the brief moments of peace that did get inserted in her life never seemed to be good enough. Either the blood pressure meter was broken, or her blood pressure was still high even with consistent medication. An actual date with her husband had been a nice change of pace, trying to repair the broken fellowship his bout with the hornets of anger had unleashed. He shared that he had stopped playing some of the games that he had been playing and some of what he had been doing, and it had been like going through withdrawals from an addiction.

Reba Jean spent some time in the sunshine and with the dogs, but it all just made her itch and wish for some time alone. Writing the book was supposed to be her way to escape, yet it just left her feeling stressed. She decided to go up to the library and see what was left. Her blood pressure was already high; she would die when God was ready for her to.

Climbing the stairs taxed what little bit of strength and energy she had; the puppy jumped on her legs the entire time. It wanted to be carried, but she ignored it as she was getting in the habit of doing. Her husband was supposed to take care of the clinginess of the puppy, too. She could hear the soothing hymns, but they only seemed to assuage the surface of her soul. She opened the door and saw everything still in tatters; the library looked like the aftermath of a nuclear fallout.

She wandered around not really doing anything; she felt more like a tourist than the owner of the establishment. Spying something that seemed strange and out of place, she came toward the old, rugged table. Right next to the oil lamp, she saw a large tome; it looked like it had come from her library, yet it seemed sinister. She saw the orangey-red title enflamed across its cover and spine, *Book of Regrets*. What was this? She didn't remember a book like this unless it was one of those in that scary aisle that she had ventured down a few weeks back.

Reba Jean slowly picked up the book almost like she was under a hypnotic influence and opened the page. It was dedicated to her and the life she could have had and signed with a sinister flourish by Insidious, the original owner of the library. She felt as if the pages burned her at their touch, yet she couldn't seem to put it down either. She watched the orange words glow, lift themselves off the page, encircle her hands, and crawl up her arms like fire ants. Every letter of regret seemed to emblazon itself on her skin like a brand from the pit of hell.

She didn't even cry out at the pain, only winced and seemed to accept that this too was her fault. She deserved this; in fact, these were her regrets. She never realized they had been recorded in a book. A tear coursed down her cheek, but the saltiness of it only seemed to ignite the fiery words into a deeper entrenchment down into her very soul it seemed. The hymn "Nearer My God to Thee" came through the airwaves, and she heard a harsh cackle advance toward her.

Peering through the dim light in the library, Reba Jean saw the huge figure of a creature march toward her. No, it wasn't Captain Insidious; it was his ranking officer, General Nefarious. The cackle grew louder as General Nefarious saw the words of regret branding Reba Jean almost like fiery chains imprisoning her. He heard the sounds of hope and help trying to wing their way to her, but she seemed to be unable to absorb the help they offered her. "Ahh, so the King tries to send you whispers of hope; He won't even come to your aid with something substantial, just song lyrics," scoffed General Nefarious.

"You are bound by your own thoughts and words, your own chains of discontent," he snidely explained. "The Great King won't help you; you mean nothing to Him." The general furthered his verbal barrage. "That music is all He gives you," he laughed with derision. Reba Jean bowed her head in defeat, but the words to the song could not be ignored. She couldn't help but focus on the one bit of help that the Holy King had sent. "When I Survey the Wondrous Cross" was the hymn that was streaming through the muck and the mire of her life. Her focus had been on her physical and emotional issues, her spiritual life was a shambles, but God Almighty still reminded her that it was to be about Him.

"Love so amazing, so divine, demands my soul, my life, my all," ended the song. She felt her very heart grab, and she stopped and realized that the hymns playing, as always were straight from the Throne of God and they were exactly what she needed to hear when she needed to hear them. Her pulse quickened; who cares about high blood pressure? She felt eagerness flow through her being. The Great King of Heaven had just told her that she was loved by Him, and she needed to remember Whose she was, and that all of her belonged to Him.

The bands of reproach and regret snapped off her, and the shards exploded back into General Nefarious' face stabbing him like missiles. The loud sounds of Amazing Grace echoed off the library walls, and Reba Jean felt life coursing back into her! She grabbed the Golden Sword that seemed to be just within reach at that very moment she needed it. She took the symbol of the Word of God and advanced upon General Nefarious. Then the words "Be Still" came into her being and she stopped.

With an unearthly howl, General Nefarious saw his chance. He swiped around the golden sword and managed to poke Reba Jean on her face. It left marks but did not go in deep. Then, as the puppy whined at her feet, she waited for the Lord to tell her what to do next, or to fight the battle for her. The words from Ephesians 6 came to mind, she needed the shield of faith, and the secret weapon of prayer. She touched the wound on her cheek, and picked up the whining dog half impatiently, but she was going to stand her ground.

The melody to "Holy, Holy, Holy" began to play, she calmed her heart and began to pray. General Nefarious began to understand how Captain Insidious had felt in here. This environment was not conducive to evil abounding. The golden lyrics of the song playing began to come towards him, he smelled the sickening sweet odor of prayer and knew that he needed to "scram!" He felt that if he left then maybe he could still come back through the doorway between the two libraries. He needed to leave before he too was banished forever.

Reba Jean inhaled deeply; the air already smelled better in the library. Boy, was this place a wreck! She did not know where Lady Jane was, probably in the conservatory, but Reba

Jean knew she had business to do if Lady Jane was going to be able to live in peace. The music changed to "Great is They Faithfulness" and she felt tears again prick her eyes. She rubbed the sore spot on her face again, scratching at it, and knew it was time to have a real time of prayer with her Heavenly Father. "All I have needed, Thy hand hath provided..." reverberated through her library. She stayed still and let the words become her prayer.

Reba Jean fell to the floor on her knees as the continued hymns became words of prayer. She poured out her heart to her Heavenly Father, asking Him to take all the regrets, stress, sin, strife, and life issues, her health all of that and cleanse and purify her of anything that did not please Him. The words of praise seemed to wrap her in a healing embrace. She had not necessarily been still and waited on the Lord; she had been a whining, complaining child much like the Israelites of old.

She crawled over to the couch cushion strewn on the floor and curled up on it with the puppy. She needed help with this zoo; it was keeping her from her prayer closet and breeding discontentment. Her husband would be home soon, and she needed to make sure there was honey oozing around, not angry hornets. "Let the Amen, sound from His people again..." intoned in her mind through the hymn that was playing. Each song that came on in succession seemed to be exactly and completely accurately orchestrated by God.

She blew her running nose on a tissue tucked into her skirt, and still felt like more prayer was needed. God was speaking to her, she was still, but she felt like she was supposed to do or say more. Reba Jean decided to do as the song was stating, thank Him and praise Him, let the Amen sound throughout the library and her life. Amen meant "so be it, or as the Lord wills," so may her life resound with an AMEN to what the Lord wanted to do with her. She felt more tears as the strains of "How Great Thou Art" began over the sound system.

Reba Jean sat on the couch cushion with the shivering dog who just wanted to nap. She prayed more and wondered if she just needed to make the living room couch her prayer closet instead of the private room that she never seemed to get to stay in very long. The continued loop of spiritual songs and hymns each spoke to her, and she began to feel a semblance that things might be healing and getting back on a spiritual even keel.

General Nefarious made it back through the adjacent library and headed to Nether Realm. He had already decided to call it a calculated retreat, so as not to appear vanquished. He wasn't; he hadn't been banished, just chased out by stupid golden notes. He didn't know why he bothered to interject into someone else's battle; he could just go wreak havoc on weaker individuals. His pride smoldered within his chest, and his anger was kindled. No, he would not be defeated by prayer and praise, he vowed.

Reba Jean continued to listen to the hymns; she was in awe of how each one in sequence was building upon the message that God seemed to be telling her specifically. Surrendering to her current conditions and realigning herself with the hope and help that He offered, she decided to stop wallowing in regret. Her chest tightened, and she surrendered her health to the Lord, she needed to stop making things worse. This stressing out over everything that annoyed her or made her tired needed to just "STOP." Not sure how to stop stressing had been stressing her! She laid her head down, closed her eyes, and just listened to the Lord speaking through the songs playing throughout the library and living room sound systems.

Chapter 15

Lady Jane was in hiding; the battle of the bees had left her scared, and the destruction in the library and Reba Jean acting like a zombie was more than she could bear. She tried to hide in the portico of peace, but her bee stings just irritated her in its breeze. She wanted to be as far away from Sir Theo's library as possible. Casting around for different escape routes, she ran to the music room out of desperation. The music was exactly what she needed; she closed her eyes and forgot about everything. King Abba sent healing words and hope through that music; it was a balm to her burdened being.

She felt whispering touches as the Overseer tended to her wounds, and she inhaled the sweet odor of prayer that seemed to permeate the chamber. She wasn't praying, so it must be that Reba Jean was here and praying earnestly. This idea alone was a boon to her spirits. The very song, "Take it to the Lord in Prayer" began and she felt as if the Lord was telling HER to pray too! Yes, if the avatar of the library wanted peace, she needed to join the mistress of the living room in prayer.

The golden lyrics caressed them in a loving embrace, as the music continued to draw them closer to the Father. Lady Jane sank to the floor on her face and entwined her prayer with Reba Jean's. The music swelled into a glorious crescendo of hope and peace filling and overflowing the library. Misty tendrils held their position in hushed adoration; the golden dust motes glittered like a galaxy of brilliant stars; the artifacts all gleamed and shimmered. The sweet sounds swirled through the whole library and as if by an unseen hand the damage and destruction were repaired, and the library was restored to its divine purpose.

Reba Jean could feel the change happening in her and around her as she continued to focus on the hymns and the subsequent prayer. Fellowship with her Father was being restored; oh, she earnestly begged for it to last. She did not want to be the foolish woman who tore her own house down; she needed to be the one that let wisdom build it. She remained curled up on the couch cushion, hoping she would not end up in some unfortunate place. Peeking through her eyelashes, she saw that yes, indeed, she was still on the couch, and all the cushions and pillows were where they were supposed to be. A thankful smile stretched across her face.

As her favorite hymn softly began to play, she felt tears trickle down her cheeks. It was well with her soul, and hopefully, after today, it would be well with the rest of her, too.

The sudden barking of the big dog interrupted her time of spiritual renewal. The delivery truck had arrived, and along with it, life returned to her reality with a suddenness that she wasn't ready for. She tamped down the rising feeling of resentment, took care of the dogs, the delivery, and sweltered through a hot flash. It was time to practice the peace that she had just been given. She could still feel the residual scars from everything in the past few weeks, but she did not want that to be the focus any longer.

Reba Jean read through her book thus far; it sounded a bit disjointed, but that was how her life was, or had been. She made some edits and wondered where this journey would take her. Her self-imposed deadline had come and gone, but she also knew that if her life was not so crazy then she probably would not have as much to write about as she did. Again, she was trying to find the silver lining to all the mayhem she seemed to fall into.

She pondered over that hulking figure that had imprisoned her. He had come from her husband's library. Thus, she couldn't build an actual wall, but she sure could build a wall of prayer! She definitely needed to do better with her prayer life, and she felt the determination strengthen within her. Finding herself a bit restless, she realized the tendrils of stress were trying to form and pull at her. She had already chewed off too many fingernails in the previous days, so she forcefully calmed herself. The puppy was the next one to try to get on her nerves, but she stiffened her proverbial spine and refused to let it stress her.

The next couple of weeks were a series of victories and defeats for the weary women. The relationship with Sir Theo was tenuous at best. Sometimes, the re-building of the relationship and fellowship seemed to make progress, other times it was as if the women were his verbal punching bag. Reba Jean finally softly threatened him by declaring that maybe she needed to leave for a couple of days if that would make his ire with her lessen. She wouldn't be around to get him all frustrated. His eyes widened, and he said "NO!" He often seemed to want to pick battles and be all defensive as if she was the one attacking him when it was all in his own perception. His narcissistic tendencies were so hurtful, and she often wanted to tell him what a jerk he was. Yes, she thought it—a real jerk—although she never said it out loud. Their relationship felt tenuous, as her wariness of him was ever-present. His library was a mess, and his living room was definitely in need of repair.

Reba Jean's own living room was in much the same condition, and she ignored the mess she thought was still in the library by not going up there. Now that the misty tendrils were left to their own devices again, she knew that the library was no longer a safe place to retreat to. She could just envision the pile of books scattered all around the floors, and she also knew that horrible things were being recorded therein. She had to get the living room under control or anything she did to the library would once again just be temporary.

She had been told to worship her way out of her mess, and as she thought about that nugget of truth, a message was preached that gave her the crux of the issue. She needed to make sure that she had not left her First Love, the Lord Jesus Christ. The only way she could worship her way through this is if her worship was for the Lord and not for other things. 1 Timothy 1:17 states, "Now unto the King eternal, immortal, invisible, the only wise God, be honour and glory for ever and ever. Amen." Her real treasure in her library and living room needed to be the LORD! His beauty and splendor were to delight her, to keep her focus on Him, and this only came through repentance.

Reba Jean found her mental attacks had worsened, and she was always confessing her thoughts and asking for forgiveness. However, she got even more viciously attacked whenever she prayed, and she understood that on a certain level. Still, she could not understand why there was such wickedness pervading her heart and mind. She just wanted to be shed of it all forever. She needed real prayer, and that always seemed to be thwarted at every turn.

Lady Jane stayed in the music room; she had no other safe place to hide. She would love to curl up in the Ancient One somehow, she just had not figured out how to do that yet. Peeking out every so often she was usually assaulted by the chaotic misty tendrils, or flying books, and there seemed to be burnt orange shards of something scattered on the floor. She had no desire to add more wounds to her already battered body and psyche. Reba Jean had relieved her of her duties and made her an observer, so she was not going to clean up the library. That arduous task belonged to the one who made or allowed the mess to happen.

She rubbed the goosebumps on her arms as she tried to decide what was required of her. Reba Jean had not been back up here, and honestly, she did not really blame her. The library was becoming a shambled mess again; the treasures were hard to see through the darkness that seemed to descend and drift through the chambers. Only the glow of the oil lamp seemed to offer a measure of comfort that all was not lost. She had noted that a wall of prayer had been started at the entrance of Sir Theo's library,

130

but it too was not finished, and the construction of it seemed to be slowed by resistance from the other side.

Every time they had a victory, it was always followed by another crushing defeat. Lady Jane knew there was hope, the anchor was there somewhere in the dark suspended just beyond reach, it seemed. She had no idea if they were still hunting treasure or just trying to keep out the rats and the vermin. The rock floor did not seem as solid as it had, she hoped that was just a figment of her frayed imagination. Should she summon her mistress and make her clean up this colossal failure? Goodness and Mercy seemed to stay in the music room as well. She was thankful for their company and knew they were not the ones to clean up the library.

Lady Jane knew that if King Abba or Lord Rabboni came to visit, They would be sorely disappointed by the condition of the library, the living room, and their respective occupants. Only rarely did the mists and darkness seem to clear, and those moments were like rare gems to Lady Jane. Then, darkness would descend, and she would pull her head back into the music room and wrap the notes around her like a golden canopy of protection.

Chapter 16

Reba Jean felt as if she was on a pre-quest, the journey before the treasure hunt so to speak. She could not hunt for the treasure if she herself was not equipped for that journey. Why was it so hard to have a clean mind and heart? She rubbed her neck and felt the tiredness behind her eyes weigh her down. She truly did love the Lord, she clung to His whispers of "Be Still," she knew He would strengthen her. He always did.

She had a moment of respite, a short visit with the Lady Matilda, and realized that her dear mentor was also going through some of the same crazy stress that she was. She found comfort in that, yet knew they would both suffer for the extra responsibilities. They talked of the young librarians and hoped that their lectures would bear fruit. Reba Jean also asked her what she should expect as she reached the Lady Matilda's age. Recently, she had encountered very condescending, patronizing women of that age range. She wanted to make sure this was not a phase she would need to be wary of when the time came. Lady Matilda had never seemed to go through that, so it seemed to be a choice either of ignorance or self-righteous pride. Reba Jean had a feeling it was a result of those who felt that they had to maintain a certain level of control. It was too reminiscent of "keeping up appearances" that was so off-putting to her.

Reba Jean did a lot of second-guessing as the days progressed; she hoped that did not mean she was double-minded. Yet, the way her mind was working, her ups and downs, made her wonder. She found herself unable to form the words she was thinking and forgetting many things. Her husband said he was forgetting things as well. Was this age, or something more immediate? Her doctor's appointment was coming up soon; she had to go, although she did not expect to get actual answers or workable solutions.

Her face would almost clear up and she would lose some weight only to gain it all back and her face looked like a teenager's. Reba Jean did not want to spend her last days on earth full of regrets or stress. Was stress obstructing her focus on the Lord and on worshipping Him? Rubbing her pock-marked face, she needed to stop the mental recriminations and get ready for work. Her quest now just seemed to be how to stop stressing and how to let God work out her life His way. Maybe that was the actual treasure hunt. The real treasures were waiting over Yonder, and King Jesus was all she needed to be looking for.

Holding her jaw firmly in her hand, she tried to still her thoughts and meditate on this. Her focus was so disjointed. The verbal barrages from her husband, her overly busy schedule, her regrets and resentment all seemed to be vying for her focus. The upcoming family events felt like an imminent trip to the gallows. Studying the book of Numbers now reinforced her study of Leviticus which left her feeling so unworthy and unclean before a Holy God. However, it had changed her perspective on her first job of serving the Lord. She was thankful to have a small part to serve Him with, she ignored the physical effect it had on her body and tried to focus on working for the ministry of the Lord.

She also decided that she would let God handle the rest of her responsibilities, and that helped her handle things a bit better. Reba Jean felt more settled in her heart as she made herself wait on the Lord. Waiting on the Lord literally also had the definition of serving the Lord. As she set her jaw to the task ahead, she cleaned the house before work and pondered many of her issues. The vacuum cleaner gave her such a strong spiritual application, that she was taken aback at the truths she saw in that simple household chore. She was like that vacuum cleaner; the dirt and debris lay all around her in need of a cleaning, yet when she vacuumed it up, she rarely dumped the canister out until it was overflowing or spitting the dirt back out onto the floor. That was her life right now, she would clean it up of sorts, and things would look tidy, but she never cleaned out the reservoir that contained all the dirt and filth. That's exactly what she needed to do, instead of carting it around and letting it linger in her life even contained in a canister of sorts.

Wandering out to the porch for a bit of contemplation, she pondered some more and a strong urge to fast came over her. Fasting was something she had always struggled with and rarely succeeded at. The realization that the overwhelming attacks might be thwarted with fasting and prayer made her determined to fast. Just that determination seemed to be a turning point for her that day. Work started out very well, but soon her low blood sugar or whatever it was commenced, and she got woozy and irritable. Reba Jean, however, stuck with it. She turned on the beautifully orchestrated hymns during her break time and was again reminded that this was war, not just a battle. She needed to understand that a war consisted of constant battles with little reprieve, and even though the war was already won, the battles still needed to be gone through. The enemy had to be defeated in her own life every day.

Listening to the hymns, she thought more upon her marriage. Was it possible that the reason she was so wary of her husband and his verbal venom was that she had yet to forgive him for the recent attacks stemming from his stress? She had technically made him acknowledge that he was wrong, and he had given offhanded apologies, but she had not in her heart forgiven him. She felt that strike her to her soul, and her heart fluttered and beat faster. She needed to forgive him and let it go; the wounds would not heal if she kept storing them and letting them fester. She felt tears well up as she surrendered her wounded heart and feelings to the Lord, asking Him to help her forgive her husband.

The week went by, and Reba Jean grew angry with herself. She kept having wicked, vile thoughts and she was sick of them! She sat down and gave herself a stern internal inspection. What she discovered was that the vile thoughts from earlier in the year and been replaced with similar but different ones. Then she realized they were triggered by stress, specifically the zoo, and then by the second job she had taken on without prayer. So, stress was the trigger, but how do you deal with stress? As the week progressed into the weekend, she realized that finally all thoughts had subsided except one, and she was determined to conquer that one before she went back to work.

Tearing up the stairs, she slammed open the library door, with a mixture of frustration, anger, and determination she began cleaning the library. The bookshelves were straightened, and any books that were not pleasing to the Lord were ruthlessly ripped from cover to cover and set in a pile in the atrium. She was going to have a real book burning! Spying some of those locked crates holding more abominable thoughts and tendencies, she dragged them into the center of the atrium. She stormed through every chamber, looking for wayward thoughts. She swatted at the dangling misty tendrils until they shrunk away from her.

With a rough yank at the hemline of her skirt, she tore off a swatch and dipped it into the fountain. With the rag full of living water, she began to wash the library from top to bottom. Reba Jean had had enough, more than enough. She would deal with the misty tendrils as soon as she prayed about how to secure them permanently. Ignoring Lady Jane's incredulous expression, Reba Jean kept up the momentum and it wasn't long before she resembled a whirling dervish. The hymn that was currently playing reached a loud crescendo, and in the subsequent pause, she could hear the pages of the Ancient One turning. Reba Jean and Lady Jane walked over to the beloved Book of the Ages. Golden words lifted off the page from Galatians 5:16, "This I say then, Walk in the Spirit, and ye shall not fulfil the lust of the

136

flesh." A few pages flipped forward to Colossians 3:5, "Mortify therefore your members which are upon the earth; fornication, uncleanness, inordinate affection, evil concupiscence, and covetousness, which is idolatry:" The ladies looked at each other with their eyes widened in recognition. These vile wicked thoughts and mental images were from the evil lust of the flesh. More pages turned reaffirming the Scripture that they already read. Just like the thought of killing herself or others, it was not anything she would do, but the flesh and the devil wanted to wear her down and defeat her in her mind.

Their hearts fluttered with the realization of the source, and yet Reba Jean also felt as if she had just been hugged, briefly. She turned to Lady Jane, stroked her arm with compassion, then turned and continued to inspect the library with a critical eye. She had started out on this journey looking for treasure and had run into a series of death traps and snares along the way.

Captain Insidious and General Nefarious put their villainous heads together and discussed the current condition of their barrage on the library. The subject of the chameleon company was again re-visited. Chameleons were such odd creatures; they liked to camouflage themselves to blend in, they had eyes that pointed in different directions, and they had long tongues. They were the epitome of Carnal Christians. However, it was noted that the dragonfly, the fly, and the bees seemed to make better spies. The target seemed to be very adept at spotting the chameleon scouts and disregarding their sly attacks. The murder hornets mixed in with the docile bees had been their strongest victory to date.

A small gnat landed near his ranking officers to report that the library seemed to be under attack from within by Reba Jean herself. The two underworld officials looked skeptical but then began to cackle derisively. How typical; most so-called Christians were very self-destructive without any help from the Nether Realm. Oh, they would take credit for the demise of the library, but the ladies would do the hard work for them. Rubbing their hands together with sinister glee, they sat down and put their feet up to await the news of the library's final destruction. To be sure, they did want to live and reign there, but to see it burn up in what amounted to a dumpster fire would be just as satisfying.

Reba Jean felt relieved to finally realize the source of her vile thoughts were from the lust of the flesh, triggered by stress. Now, she needed to find a way to deal with stress. There were moments of total relaxation, but she found that she still kept herself from fully relaxing, like she was waiting for the next thing to happen. She knew this stemmed from anxiety. Whether it was from the last couple of weeks or a life of emotional trauma, she needed to find a way to truly enjoy the gift of peace and joy that had been given to her by the Lord.

The next couple of weeks were going to be so busy, she also knew that she needed to somehow not react as the hurt little girl she had been for so many years when the family came together for their reunion. Reba Jean sat down on the edge of the settee, but her left leg bounced rapidly, a signal that she was restless and had much to resolve. Acid rose in her throat; her supper was not sitting well with all this anger and harried running around. She forced her leg to stop its rapid up-and-down movement, she inhaled, and tried to slow her breathing.

Lady Jane timidly sat down next to her mistress, and with a wary expression, she watched to see what Reba Jean would decide to do next. She half thought that maybe things had been better when she was the supervisor of this place. Then she remembered how the books targeted her and she was always feeling bruised and battered. Ever since she had discovered the portico of peace, she could usually escape anything in the library. The murder hornets had been the only exception to that respite. Lady Jane found herself longing to go to the portico; she grabbed Reba Jean's hand and pulled her down the corridor and out to the side portico.

Reba Jean sat on the swing. She began to daydream and found herself drifting off into relaxation. She had had many amazing spiritual applications come to her while on her own patio swing. She even considered the idea of writing a little book called Porch Ponderings. The orchestrated music seemed to cover her like a soothing blanket. She could feel it healing torn places in her soul and mind. This might be a way for her to fully relax if she let it take effect before she became antsy again.

She rubbed her face and smeared around the healing salve that she had put on it. She was determined to clean up her pockmarked face. Scrubs, ointments, and cleansings all needed to be used regularly, and this, too, applied spiritually and mentally. Reba Jean had changed her hair, and although she liked it, she now felt it made her look even more like her mother. That really bothered her, and she cast about mentally for ways to look like a child of God and not a by-product of a failed human union.

Still feeling nauseous, Reba Jean hugged Lady Jane and left her on the swing. Returning to the living room, she went to take an antidote for her stomach. The puppy was playing with its favorite feline who so patiently let it wrestle and attack it with a vengeance. The patience of the cat was so sweet to watch as the puppy persistently tried to get the upper hand. Reba Jean pondered if there were any spiritual parallels she could draw from that scenario. Was she the puppy, or was she the patient cat? Honestly, she could see her filling both roles, and that made her discard that train of thought.

Reba Jean meandered up and down the hallway; her hubby was relaxing in his office playing one of his games. Their relationship seemed to be settling down; they both had to watch how they reacted to each other. She had found herself wanting to fuss at him earlier today and tell him off for no real reason. She had stopped herself, and when he had gotten a bit snippy with her later, she did not retaliate, just soothingly replied. It was progress, and progress was good. He had come to bed last night and was reading the Bible. He was also reading his book on prayer and looking to get involved again in church. All of these were huge answers to prayer.

One issue had been ferreted out and was being put right, but what about her prayer closet issue? She was so angry that she had no place to truly get alone with God and pray as she used to and how she longed to. Sitting at the table in the kitchen, Reba Jean slowly turned her head and mind around her house, asking God to help her find a place for a prayer closet. Oh, she had a few options, but the zoo or her own brain were often huge distractions in the places she had previously chosen. Distractions were the real pitfall to her spiritual growth lately, and she was desperate to have victory of that which caused such defeat.

As if on cue, the puppy barreled over to her and jumped up against her leg. She touched its head but then ignored it, and it ran off. Inwardly, she was sending up little prayers for help in a solution to the prayer closet issue. Yes, this was a big deal to her, and it was probably her own fault for the zoo being a distraction. Reba Jean was going to persistently pursue this to a victorious end, and then her treasure hunt would be more successful.

Looking at the time, Reba Jean was surprised to see the night was racing along closer to bedtime. This had been her only real day off, had she squandered it? Why did it take so long for her to settle down and relax? Even a brief daydream on a porch swing had not been treasured as it should have been. Reba Jean decided to rejoin Lady Jane in the portico off the library's side.

Chapter 17

Reba Jean took imaginary trips to her library over the next few months; she had tried to stay out of there as much as possible in hopes that the murder hornets would leave Lady Jane alone. The first book had been printed and was out for distribution. She had learned a lot in that process, it was quite the eye opener of her own thought processes concerning topics on mental health and ingrained subconscious reactions to those who had disorders.

The second book had not been written in for months, but the treasure hunt had been intense and fruitful. Reba Jean furiously took notes and absorbed the treasures that were to be found in her devotions, using books by well-known or trusted authors, messages from church sermons, and meditation on God's Word. The resounding theme had been "Be still and know that He is God." Although, she had wanted to write and finish Book Two months ago, she would have totally missed out on the treasures she had found in the meantime.

Sir Theo whisked her off for a week away from the zoo with an admonition to rest and work on the book only as God allowed. Reba Jean remembered how she had wanted to set fire to the whole library and just burn it all down. The only thing that had stopped her was knowing that Lady Jane might get hurt in that horrific plan. Shoving back the hair that flopped in her face, she debated whether she should check on the library after all this time?

The possibility that the murder hornets might have set up a hive between the doorway to Sir Theo's library and her own was a likely scenario. She knew that some nefarious minion of the underworld was sure to have found a crack to build a strong hold in using that space. The scar tissue from the previous attacks had been the perfect webbing to use for connecting the underworld to the two libraries. Purposing in her heart not to react incorrectly to such attacks, she continued to build a wall of prayer around the entrance to Sir Theo's library.

With dogged determination, she began to study how to react to the verbal onslaught that stress and personal preferences manufactured. "Be angry and sin not" was often quoted under her breath. RATS and murder hornets needed to be exterminated, and peace and patience needed to replace them.

A short time later, Reba Jean reluctantly ascended the long staircase to the library; she felt the weight of every step and it seemed so exhausting just to reach the door. She tried to open the door to the library; was it supposed to push inwardly, or pull outwardly? She puzzled at this; why did the opening of the door seem so confusing after all this time. Did it open differently in the past? Reba Jean was getting befuddled, and trying not to be impatient; she shoved open the door with a concentrated burst of exertion.

Stumbling into the door that had just opened barely a crack, she tried to squeeze into the sliver of an opening. It was extremely dark, and the air felt heavy and cloying. Mystified, Reba Jean pushed harder into the library using all her strength. She fell flat on her face onto the cool floor tiles of the atrium. The darkness had not dissipated, but as she looked around the tiles, she saw spots that glowed golden even in the darkness. Crawling like some sort of sea creature along the floor she navigated to the first golden glow. She touched the glowing floor tile and felt hope surge through her fingers. Her eyes grew enlarged in wonderment, and she slid her fingers onto the next tile ahead of it and sure enough that one glowed. With a catch of her breath, she slowly spread hope and light to each tile so that she could see a path ahead as she crawled forward through the library. She wasn't sure where she was headed or what she would find, but she had hope that lit her way as she went.

After a few minutes of this, she stopped to get her bearings and to give her knees a break from the arduous crawling she had been doing on the hard tile. The library was very still, the denseness of the misty tendrils was overbearing. Yet, there did not seem to be a sense of evil or danger, in fact, it felt very quiet, and peace filled. She looked around and saw the golden path of hope behind her, and golden spots randomly placed in front of her. She also saw some hot lava-colored stones beckoning her off the side of the path. Reba Jean sat still and chose not to move as she considered what her eyes were observing. The lava stones were obviously paths she could choose that would be full of anger and discontentment and selfishness. She had been down such paths before, and those always led to destruction. She wanted to find the Ancient One, the Lamp, the Golden Swords, and Lady Jane. She decided to stay on this path of Hope, knowing it would lead her to the Anchor of her soul.

With a glance at the stones of lava, she started crawling again spreading the golden glow to each tile ahead of her as she searched out the path to follow. It was not an easy task, she had to sit still many times whilst fighting against impatience and doubt. She blew out a huge breath and as the misty tendrils fluttered in response, she caught a breathtaking view of a beautiful treasure room ahead of her in the area that she had estimated the Ancient One to be on Its beautiful marble pedestal.

Gasping with wonder and fatigue, Reba Jean sat for a moment. Closing her eyes, a wisp of a hymn drifted into her thoughts. "Breathe on me, O breath of God…" Her eyes widened yet again as a thought came to mind, and acting upon that thought, she whispered the words, "Breathe on me, O breath of God…" Tears sprang to her eyes, and her body went limp in response to the loveliest breeze that blew through that library in response to her whispered prayer. The misty tendrils were blown up into the rafters again, and the darkness dissipated with their absence. The air was fresh and flowery, and there in front of her were treasures heaped around the Ancient One. Reba Jean cried in thankfulness and relief.

Even though she had not been in the library, the treasures she had collected down in the living room had been piling up there, too. Falling forward on her face, she began to sing "All hail the power of Jesus' Name, let angels prostrate fall…" Reba Jean began to worship King Abba and Lord Rabboni right there with her face on the golden tiles of the library. She praised, prayed, pondered, and then without intending to she fell into a peaceful sleep.

Lady Jane felt a huge refreshing breeze blow through the library, it had been dark for months since Reba Jean had stopped visiting. It wasn't always a scary darkness, but it had been fraught with doubt, insecurity, loneliness, and questions. The rats had nibbled at her ankles, and the murder hornets had stung her furiously at times. She would often feel butterfly wings brush against her like a reassuring whisper that all hope was not lost.

Lady Jane had hidden in the music room until that too had become still and mostly silent. Crawling her way back to the portico, she curled into a protective position on the swing and waited to see what would become of all this. Now, months later, that breeze offered hope and help; she reached forward as if it was an extended hand and let it draw her back to the main library. Arriving at the Ancient One, she spied in the wonderful golden glow that peaceful form of Reba Jean asleep on the tiled floor.

Lady Jane looked in awe at the beautiful treasures stacked around, that had been hidden by the darkness. Her self-imposed seclusion caused her to miss months of knowing these treasures were even here! Lady Jane sank down to the floor and stroked the treasures within reach with trembling fingers. Hope, peace, joy, thankfulness, prayer, praise, she half laughed, half cried as she felt these very treasures surge into her being as she touched them.

Reba Jean stirred and saw Lady Jane aglow with wonder and delight on the floor nearby. Her fingers were stroking the treasures and you could see the very attributes pulsating through her body. Together, they explored and examined the treasures that had been stored up around them. Spying a couple of tiny groupings, they found that long suffering and patience were there but only in small amounts. These treasure piles needed to be built up higher as they were so vital to the survival of the library and its residents.

Grabbing each other's hands, the two women toured the library which was no longer shrouded in darkness. Going along the corridor of hope, they soon arrived at a beautiful nursery with a precious baby laying therein, an answer from much prayer. They slowly exited and felt a longing to visit the music room. It was quiet and still in that room, yet they felt the praise music and heard it coursing through their very being. Turning to face each other, they silently wondered at this change. The music was there, but it wasn't in the room, it was in them!

Skipping along corridors they spotted all the beloved artifacts still in their places and felt such peace and contentment permeate the very air they breathed. Passing the tv room they saw that it had shrunk to just a grotto sized space. Reba Jean was purposing not to watch much tv, and even her time on social media was yet again very limited. Their steps led them towards Sir Theo's library entrance, and both of them held each other's hands tightly and felt trepidation seep into their pores.

Reba Jean had heard that a young lady named Skye had read the first book and had mentioned that she didn't think Reba Jean liked her husband very much. That observation had stung Reba Jean, but it was not untrue. The murder hornets had done quite the work on Reba Jean in the past few months. She realized she did not love her husband with agape love from 1 Corinthians, but now that she realized it, she knew she needed to change that.

These thoughts and memories wrapped themselves around Reba Jean like a vine of poison ivy as she headed towards the arch between the libraries. Lady Jane could feel the fear beginning to build in the two of them. The peace that she had felt in the other parts of the library seemed to be dissipating the closer they came to Sir Theo's library. Together, they tiptoed to the archway to see what would happen. Reba Jean felt her blood pressure start to rise, and she tried to still her nerves.

The closer they got the more entangled they seemed to get in that vine that irritated them with its fear and feelings of dislike and impatience. They clawed at the vine and at their skin as it inflicted sores on them. Growling fiercely, they managed to get untangled and fell into a heap in the archway between the two libraries. Looking around they saw eyes glowing at them between cracks, the reddish orange orbs seemed to shoot daggers of anger and hate at them. There in the cracks in the archway were the horrid murder hornets living, ready for attack at any moment.

Reba Jean caught herself whimpering, and she thought she would just shrivel up there and die just at the mere thought of the vine or the hornets attacking. She felt something biting her ankle and she saw a rat had ventured out to taste her. The revulsion to these attacks was building inside of her and she screamed in frustration. She felt the same as the writer of Lamentations 1:16, "For these things I weep; mine eye, mine eye runneth down with water, because the comforter that should relieve my soul is far from me: my children are desolate, because the enemy prevailed." Then as tears slid from her eyes onto the floor, they seemed to illuminate the tiles they dropped on to. It was a reminder that she had been building a wall of prayer around the entrance to Sir Theo's library. Her Comforter was there, she just needed to cry out to Him.

Placing her hands on the floor, she began praying earnestly for Sir Theo. Lady Jane watched her mistress and noticed that as she began praying the very floor tiles seemed to strengthen, and the sides of the archway began to seal up its cracks. Glowing angry creatures seemed to shrink away and be covered with a crystalline seal. Lady Jane was in awe as she watched books begin opening in Sir Theo's library. She wandered into that library to see what the books were, books themselves were so rare in this electronic data center. Lady Jane hugged herself with happiness as she saw these were books on prayer! Surely between Sir Theo studying actual books about prayer, and Reba Jean erecting a wall of prayer, King Abba must surely be pleased to send the Overseer to their marriage to build it upon agape love.

Reba Jean sat back on her heels, and soaked in the peace that was flowing around them at this moment. She treasured this peace from God; it seemed so fragile and temporary because of the sin that so easily beset them. She would write about these treasures and how it was stated in 1 Peter 3:1 she needed to stir up "pure minds by way of remembrance." That pure mind however still needed to be achieved, but it was on the right path by remembering what she was to think upon and transforming it by renewing it daily in the Word of God.

Lady Jane and Reba Jean lingered a bit longer in the archway before moving along with their tour of the library. They saw some other corridors had formed, but they did not wish to explore these uncharted paths. Passing by the place of the old dream room, they noticed that it was just a slight indentation in the wall. The strongbox in front of it was still chained securely. The emphasis was no longer on the dreams, or the media entertainment that had seemed to control the library for years. Hand in hand, they returned to the portico they both loved so much. The air was soothing and refreshing as they flopped onto the swing and began to discuss all that they had seen on their tour. Then, their conversation backtracked to the months prior when they had been separated and disconnected.

All sense of time was lost as they caught up on their lives, their thoughts, and their feelings over the last couple of months. Reba Jean shared her spiritual battles and search for treasure that was lasting and permanent. Lord Rabboni had done so much for Reba Jean, helping her remove stress, triggers, and strongholds from her life. The abominable thoughts were much less now, and thoughts of peace, hope, and strength were built upon. Lady Jane shared how she had just hidden herself away on this very swing in the portico and waited for the end, the end of whatever this was.

Reba Jean did not know how she was even going to begin to write down everything that she had learned in the last couple of months. She had notebooks upon notebooks with an asterisk alongside every thought that she wanted to share. Reaching upward towards the misty tendrils, she tugged one and sure enough with a soft ruffle of pages, all her notes came fluttering down around her. She paged through them, showing Lady Jane the thoughts and fragments of hope and peace that she had gathered like treasure.

Lady Jane pondered these spiritual gems and tapping a finger against her cheek she posed a question to Reba Jean. "Do you think that maybe you should do a companion devotional using these Scriptures?" Reba Jean stilled herself and fastening her eyes on Lady Jane she just sat there and pondered that idea. She already knew and was approved to do Porch Ponderings, a devotional series on the spiritual applications and lessons she had already written down through the years. Many of these she used in her lectures to the librarian apprentices. Did God want her to write a devotional just about Treasure for the Heart?

Scratching her head, her face twisted into a quizzical grimace. She knew she would need to think and pray about that. The responsibility of writing a devotional was huge to her, and here she was considering writing yet another one. Rubbing her chin, she contemplated whether to just include all the Scripture in this book she was currently writing or make a separate devotional as a companion to this book. Reaching down, she picked up the first notebook that was near her just to see how many treasures were in this particular one alone. Each page seemed to open a treasure chest and beckon her to explore its contents. She could see how a devotional could be written using these notes and Scriptures.

This was too huge for a quick decision one way or the other; Reba Jean needed to pray more about this undertaking. With a tinge of restlessness, she stood up and pushed away from the swing and Lady Jane. "I think I need to go for a walk, my dear. Alone. Well not alone, but with God." Reba Jean walked back through the library, looking longingly on the treasure piles along the way. She was not sure what to do, but one thing that had become insistently clear to her was to be still and listen for God to direct her path. There she would find peace and hope along the way, even if it was fraught with danger and doubt or even discord. She exited the library, checking the door to see which way it swung.

Feeling restless still with this idea of writing a companion devotional to her second book, she made her way back to the living room. Looking around, she felt the need to go for a real walk in the big outdoors. She was still on her trip; she was not even in her home state. The hotel was peaceful and quiet, and she was so thankful that her husband had wanted her to get away from the stress of the zoo to rest, to write, to do whatever, to recharge. This was such an answer to prayer.

Reba Jean grabbed her hotel key and left the room to walk and pray. She spent some time thinking and relaxing outside. It was so peaceful that she almost fell asleep in the warm southern air. She meandered around the hotel lobby, assured in her mind that she would most likely write a companion devotional to her second book. She probably had a few more plot twists to insert and then a mountain of editing to do, but her second book was

149

nearing completion. It would have a happy ending, for much treasure had been discovered and collected along the way.

It was still early in the day, but she was so relaxed and peaceful even after writing for almost two hours that she contemplated a nap. After her nap she would leisurely get ready for dinner with family, and a reconnect with her husband who had been gone all day for work. One thing was very clear, she relished a stress-free life, no zoo, no schedule, no expectations to invade her peace. She was not sure how this could be achieved at home, however. She needed to find a way NOT to stress, not to react to other's emotions and issues, to let the peace of God rule and reign in her heart no matter the situation.

She closed her notebooks strewn around her desk, thankful for the call to remembrance that they offered. Still pondering over the treasures and the possible paths ahead, she decided to try for that nap she knew that her body needed. Rest was a treasure, surely it was to her right now. She would need to look up verses to see if the physical rest was the same as the spiritual rest. She knew that if she was spiritually rested, it would affect her physical rest too.

Reba Jean tried to nap, but the hallway was noisy, so she took a long, luxurious shower instead. *Ahh, this is the life*, she thought to herself. Still toying with the idea of writing a companion devotional, but also needing to clear her head, she meandered down to the veranda of the hotel. The deep southern breeze was soothing, and she soaked in the nothingness that she had craved for so long. Thoughts of things to write further in the book gave her a restlessness that disrupted her relaxation. When she was away from the library, all she could think of was the library and the books that she wanted to write. When she was in front of the laptop it seemed increasingly difficult to articulate all the thoughts and scenarios that she had just mentally orchestrated minutes prior.

Chapter 18

Conte' was put to task again, not that the cat-like creature minded. Conte' was from a family of minions that just seemed to have nine lives. When one was banished, another one was available to take its place. He seemed harmless enough as he wove around the corners of Reba Jean's subconsciousness. She was trying to be content and enjoy the luxury of this respite from the normal stresses that her home life produced and exacerbated. He purred in sheer devilish enjoyment to be on active duty especially down here on "vacation." His master would be pleased to hear that Reba Jean was restless and struggling to know what to do or what path to take.

Careful not to overly alert her to his presence, he would wander away just long enough out of sight for her to relax her guard and begin to enjoy his absence. Then, just when she was peaceful and relaxed, he would wrap his itchy tail around her leg or arm or rub his bewhiskered face against hers and cause that mild burst of irritation that seemed to come out of nowhere.

Conte' watched as Reba Jean wandered around the hotel, up and down the floors, lobby, verandas, and her room all the while trying to hang onto that fleeting peace that she had felt earlier. He growled under his breath when across the sound waves could be heard her thoughts "godliness with contentment is great gain." He must not have been as careful as he had thought for her to start quoting Scripture in her head.

Reba Jean felt tired still and fought the restless feeling that seemed to have descended upon her. She sat down to write more in the book about treasures to store in one's library. No rats, tendrils, vines, or other nefarious creatures seemed to disturb her, but she could not shake that restless feeling that seemed to brush against her in frequent intervals. She was hungry, but there was nothing to eat; she was tired, but could not sleep. The television had no appeal to her, which was good. Being outside only made her more restless and sleepier. She did not think she was bored, per se, but there just seemed to be something niggling at her.

Her fingers pounded on the keyboard as she typed along, but her thoughts were not as cohesive as she had hoped. Looking around the desk at all the books and notes that she had brought that represented the storehouse of treasure that she had accumulated in the last few months, she was thankful, but felt like something was missing. Mentally listing the treasures that had become her faithful companions, she began to check them off as if they were on a list. She had peace, faith, prayer, and praise. Out of those, prayer was the most precious to her, but all the others came because of prayer and prayer came because of the others. They were all interwoven like a chain of fine gold. Friends that impacted her spiritually were another treasure that she had recently realized she had. Lady Constance greatly impacted her spiritual growth, and she had become a real treasure to Reba Jean.

Sunshine had encouraged her to write the devotionals, to express the treasure that could be found in Scripture that was more precious than life itself. She was grateful for her husband growing in the Lord; their talks about what they were learning and reading were a treasure to her. Miss Skye would be pleased to note that the marriage was really improving as long as they kept their differences from overcoming their spiritual bonding.

Reba Jean knew that contentment just wasn't growing, it seemed to be in the same category as patience, and long suffering. Such tiny little spots that could have great potential if she would just collect more of each. She paused and decided to do a study on contentment, just to see if it settled her restlessness. As she studied this out, she realized why contentment seemed to be in the same area as patience and long suffering, and she also realized that why she was low on these attributes was because she had filled her life with anger, frustration, and irritation. Now that she was trying to remove these, the space or void they left felt empty or at least not filled with much. That produced the restlessness she was feeling. She always tried to fill that emptiness with food, tv, social media, reading, anything to keep the spots from feeling empty.

Conte' cringed and shrunk back as the closeness of the light from the Scriptures began to shine on him. He did not want that holy essence touching and burning him! Neither did he want Reba Jean to realize that he was the one feeding her subconscious with restless thoughts and feelings. DisCONTEntment shrunk back into his itchy self and slid off into a corner to return at another time.

Reba Jean pondered what she had read about grace, happiness, and trusting God and surmised that she was antsy because she hadn't learned how to be filled with the right stuff. She twirled around in her desk chair munching on M&Ms, and pondering the extent of her discontentment. Expelling a sigh, she wondered if she should get ready for tonight or go wander the hotel again expending excess restlessness.

Seriously though, what was causing her to be so restless she wondered? She was writing after all these months; she knew she would have devotionals to write when she returned home. She truly was enjoying the time here, and time itself seemed to slow down so that she could appreciate it. Did she have unconfessed sin? Was she feeling the frustration of her physical expectations or her perception of things? She tried to pray to seek answers from God, but there just seemed to be silence. *OH!!* That's right, she needed to calm down, be still, and wait on the Lord. She would, of course, be anxious and restless when she wasn't waiting on Him, because that is tied to patience, long suffering, and contentment. She sucked in air and blew it out in a gusty exhale; enough of this restlessness!

Working on her hair for dinner that evening, she was frustrated as usual with her appearance. She had not been contented with the style or color that she had longed for and received. Her skin was still having sores from its contact with radiation and stress. Innermost feelings of ugliness threatened to overwhelm her. Once her hair was tamed to some sort of semblance of decency, she went to work on her face trying to look attractive. She was not one for much makeup, just enough to cover the angry blemishes and supposedly to enhance her features. She had not packed all her makeup, and now wished that she had. She wasn't sure who she was trying to impress; her family rarely made her feel attractive, although her husband appreciated it when she looked less than ghoulish.

Reba Jean walked away from her fastidious fussing and hoped that a few minutes away from the mirror would somehow change her appearance or her perception thereof the next time she viewed herself. Was her appearance, the outward man causing this discontentment? She sure had been full of it lately, everything she did in hopes to look more attractive had not satisfied her. She knew the hair would grow out and change. She was losing weight. And her skin would heal if she took care of it. Was it more a reflection of her inner self? Did she have weight of besetting sin, dead or sore flesh, recalcitrant tendrils of something that detracted from Jesus shining through?

The night of fellowship had been full of laughs and no mention of appearances, good or bad. She had probably made too much of a personal issue out of how she had looked. However, a night of restlessness, night sweats, and hot flashes caused a lack of sleep. She forced herself not to react wrongly to anything because she knew her physical condition could exacerbate everything said or done. As she reluctantly walked the path outside, she asked God why she was so discontented and what she should do about it.

Reba Jean returned to her hotel room and began her personal Bible Study time. Every book she read, every Scripture was completely aimed at her question of discontentment. It was sobering to realize that her discontentment was of her own making, of possibly even questioning God about why she looked the way she did, or the family He had put her into at birth. She was questioning God's sovereignty whilst expecting grace and even permission to be grouchy.

Reba Jean paused and confessed her discontentment and grumpy attitude to the Lord. Even if she had any valid reasons, they were moot in sight of how she was to react, to respond to the issues of life. Running her fingers through her tangled mop of hair, she humbled herself before God and asked forgiveness for not submitting to His plan for her life. It did not matter if she had some Syndrome, or OCD, or any other sort of mental or physical disorder; it should never make her doubt that God had a perfect plan and purpose for her life. So, what if she wasn't outwardly attractive? That was not to be her goal in life.

Her discontentment came from not being satisfied with the goodness of God, as she had studied about this morning. She was not looking for the good trees in her garden. She was always focused on the tree she was not supposed to eat from. It was time to retrain her focus onto all the blessings God had bestowed upon her. She could not even count them all or write them all down, so why hone in on the few things that she wished were different? Reba Jean gulped and felt her body shiver as the impact of this washed over her.

The same old restless feeling tried to disturb her; she almost jumped up to pace around, but that was not going to accomplish anything. She sat still and let the Holy Spirit continue His transforming work in her mind and heart. A tendril of hair tried to irk her, and she blew it off her forehead emphatically. She ran her hands back through her unruly mop and determined not to be so self-conscious about how she looked. She was the caretaker of this body, this garden, but she was NOT the Owner. She would take care of it, but not obsess about how it was supposed to look or be different.

Reba Jean sat still and meditated on her studies that morning, and as she did so she felt the focus change from her discontentment to submission to God's will for her life. However, she still felt the fatigue settle in; she hoped she would be able to take a good nap this afternoon. Little anxious thoughts kept knocking at her mind's door and she kept ignoring them. No, she did not feel well, but she refused to add to her weakened system with heaps of anxious thoughts.

The jiggling of her leg told her that her subconscious was still at odds with her spiritual determination to be different. She contemplated taking a nap right then in hopes that it would quell her issues for today. After trying to rest, Reba Jean gave up and took a shower before walking over to the mall to buy stuff to tame her hair and eat a healthy lunch. Putting her hair up fixed that annoying issue; she should have packed more hair stuff from her personal stash at home. Lesson learned the hard way, but still learned for the future.

Reba Jean caught up on news and messages, synced with her husband, and chilled on the couch in the hotel room. She wasn't sure how much more writing was left in her book before she would consider it completed, she really wanted to send it off to the publishers upon her return home. She really hoped they would approve it and begin the publishing process. Her whole attitude and mental attitude had changed from earlier, surrender of her own discontentment had mellowed her out. It was a relief not to feel restless and antsy for once.

Chapter 19

General Nefarious and Captain Insidious had been watching Reba Jean for a while. The last few months had been quite the entertaining escapade for them. They had been able to insert murder hornets into Sir Theo's gentle bees and used them repeatedly to viciously attack Reba Jean and Lady Jane. They had dispatched the Chameleon Company until Reba Jean got so paranoid, she thought everyone around her was a chameleon. Lately, Conte' had seemed to have the most effect on Reba Jean, causing her consistent frustration about little petty things. Their favorite attack was using a poisonous vine to release its toxins into Reba Jean physically and mentally.

Both of the nether world minions chortled with diabolical glee as they recounted the various ways, they had managed to attack the library and its caretaker and mistress without even stepping foot themselves in there. General Nefarious realized that he did not need to be actually inside the library to harm it. They remembered how the voyage so many months ago had given them the ability to release rats that to this day were still making victorious forays into the so-called spiritual stronghold that Reba Jean had tried to erect in the library and living room. But a hiss and growl alerted them to the return of Conte' whose disgruntled expression was enough to let them know that somehow Reba Jean had achieved victory again.

"What was it this time, my scurvy pet?" queried General Nefarious.

"Well, I was able to get past her stern mental recriminations, but the persistent prayer finally kicked me to the curb!" lamented Conte'.

"That seems to be our ongoing weakness; every time she prays, she is building a wall or tearing down our strongholds. We need to find a way to keep her from this. In the past it was easy to distract her when she prayed. Let's gather the troops and see if we can ferret out possible tools to utilize in our next attacks," barked General Nefarious.

Captain Insidious withdrew and mulled over the niggling thought that he had forgotten something. After some deep introspection, he remembered that Reba Jean had seemed to equate him to a pirate. He had determined to live up to her evil vision of himself. Pirates pillaged and stole from their victims; they were especially noted for gathering loot and valuable treasures in the middle realm. What did Reba Jean possibly treasure that would warrant her building a fortification to keep him out of the library? The last time he had been in the library, there was that Ancient One, the golden swords, the fountain, and oil lamp. He was sure she had probably rearranged some rooms and utilized the vaults and crates. He had not received any word from the murder hornets, rats, or even Conte' as to any serious changes to the library. This bore launching a serious investigation, and he needed to find just the right scout to get into the library on his behalf and report what sort of treasure that Reba Jean thought she could keep from him.

He did not share his thoughts or plans with General Nefarious; he wanted to be promoted without sharing the victory. Let General Nefarious scheme and rally the troops; he was going to command a covert operation, a real black ops. Cackling on his mental play on words, Captain Insidious cast a jaundiced eye over the likely candidates. Insecurity, Doubtful, Anxiety, Fear, and Discontent all had been useful in the past. However, it seemed that Reba Jean was able to recognize them as Evil Agents, and they were never able to stay embedded in the library. The rats, vines, and murder hornets were not smart enough or developed enough to be anything but infantry.

Captain Insidious knew that he might have to find a devious candidate in the underground network of mercenaries.

He really just wasn't sure exactly what or who he was looking for; he just expected to know it when he saw it. *What would keep Reba Jean from collecting treasure or praying? Was it more important to find out what the treasure was, or just to keep her from praying,* he wondered to himself. *Ha, that little wimp prays over everything; maybe I need to make her feel safe and give her a false sense of peace so that she won't think that she has to pray?*

What would give her a false sense of peace? Captain Insidious considered Apathy, then decided that he would still search out the unexpected secret agent for this most delicious mission yet.

He had heard through the rats that Reba Jean stressed over her family obligations and social expectations. He knew that this past summer and fall had been fraught with issues with the temporary second job, and of course the zoo. He studied his notes and realized that if a thought or situation was presented in such a way that it would seem that it should be God's will since family or church expected it of her, then she would often do it, WITHOUT praying.

This sort of situation would take skill and finesse, to deceive her into thinking she was doing the right thing as there seemed to be little wrong in it, to get her entrapped by her own desire to be a "good Christian." Captain Insidious had manufactured these in the past or had at least taken credit for her defeat. He wondered if she had truly learned her lessons after repeating the same mistakes, or if he might just be able to slide another one in where she wouldn't pray until it was basically too late.

A chameleon scout might help him know which person or situation could be manipulated, or maybe he just needed to bide his time awaiting the right opportunity. His lack of attacks might lull her into thinking she was living victoriously and forgetting to suit up in her armor and stay alert.

However, he would be wise to see what General Nefarious decided to do with his army that he had assembled. If the General had a miserable defeat, it might get him demoted, and then Captain Insidious could rise up through the ranks! He rubbed his clawed fingers together in agitated delight as he contemplated how to play both sides of the battlefield. A snippet of a Scripture verse "hope deferred maketh the heart sick;" drifting through his memory. Yes, all soldiers of the Nether Realm knew Scripture, they knew how to twist it and use it against the soldiers of the Celestial Realm. He needed to find a way to keep her from praying and from hoping that things would get better.

Chapter 20

Oh, Reba Jean sure had a surprise for Lady Jane! With a giggle that could barely be contained, Reba Jean led a special guest into the library. Together, they tiptoed down the corridor to the portico, hoping to find Lady Jane there. Peeking around the door, Reba Jean spied her sweet little avatar lounging on the swing with one foot dangling to give the swing an occasional nudge of movement. Lady Jane would be so thrilled to have a visitor that did not have to be banished from the library!

Lady Jane heard a muffled giggle and looked up in time to see two women leap at her from the doorway! Why, it was the Lady Constance! Oh, Lady Jane was overjoyed to see her dear friend and confidante right there in the library with them! Together, they sat on the swing and talked around each other. The entire portico was punctuated with exclamation points like confetti falling around them. They chatted for a while, and then their tone got a bit more serious as they began discussing the spiritual battles they had endured and the possible reasons they had not been victorious at the onset.

"Lady Constance, why do you think you suffered so many dark days of depression?" asked Reba Jean.

"Well, Reba Jean, I stopped praying and living for the Lord. I would lay around and do nothing. It became harder to do anything. I would sort of pray because I knew I had to, but with no real faith or feeling. I even read Scripture, but I did not let it change how I was feeling. Everything became so exhausting, and that was even more depressing. It was a vicious circle that kept me trapped in the dark." remembered Lady Constance. "I just gave up on life, and family, on everything, it was so dark, I did not see a way out. BUT GOD!" exclaimed Lady Constance. "You see God had not given up on Lady Constance. He saved her soul; He saved her sanity; He saved her service. What a mighty God!"

"So, how do you stay out of that darkness, now?" asked Lady Jane.

"I don't know about you, but when I pray… I don't see darkness because the Light is being called upon." replied Lady Constance. As she described the glorious Light, it descended upon them in a warm glow straight from the celestial realm. They felt themselves filled with power and strength wrapped in a loving hug of peace.

Together, the three of them went to the treasure room of the library and began discussing the collected treasures there. The celestial light followed them, and the entire library was bathed in a heavenly glow. Each treasure heap was illuminated and the precious artifacts themselves seemed to almost sing as they absorbed the light. Hearing pages of the Ancient One rustling, they wandered over to the marble pedestal and watched to see what Scripture would be selected for them. Scripture after Scripture poured out of the Ancient One like liquid gold and the air was surrounded by the beautiful, wonderful words of life. They were all the passages that Reba Jean had collected in her notes about the treasures she was to seek. With one last page flip, the Ancient One turned to Matthew 6:21, one of the very first verses that had started this treasure hunt half a year earlier. With golden words illuminated by the celestial realm the three women read aloud, "For where your treasure is, there will your heart be also."

Lady Constance began to sing in a soft voice of victory, "Look what God has done for you." As the song came to a soft reverent finish, the three friends knelt down on the glowing tiles of the atrium and thanked King Abba and Lord Rabboni for all the treasures that He had given them to value and hold dear.

Epilogue

Reba Jean found herself having bouts of anger, anger so strong that she wanted to physically lash out at her husband not just verbally. She had to exert a great amount of self-control. It seemed that every time she tried to have victory, and not react, the battle would intensify.

Editing the second book depressed her, it seemed that both books repeated themselves. She was thankful she had an editor that cared about her. The editor had offered a listening ear, or even a professional counsellor if Reba Jean felt that she needed it. Just knowing that help was there was help in and of itself.

Then her pastor made a comment in his last message that solved all of her issues. He said it was time to let the past be in the past, turn the page, finish the chapter, and close the book. He had no clue how extremely relevant this was for her. That's exactly what she did, she turned the page, finished the chapter, and closed the book on the painful past. She could either let it influence her or define her.

A week after that decision, she finished the edits on the second book, and strongly suspected she had the title for the third book in the Lady Jane Chronicles. Would it be called the Library of Influence?

www.ingramcontent.com/pod-product-compliance
Lightning Source LLC
Chambersburg PA
CBHW022129170626
46808CB00002B/909